Mao's Kisses
A Novel of June 4, 1989

Early Praise for *Mao's Kisses*

Midway through the novel Mao's Kisses, *Ge (or G), personal notetaker for Deng Xiaoping and letter writer for migrant workers, asks himself during the events leading up to the Tiananmen Square political storm,* What is the real China? *Here is the central question, examined over and over again, in Alex Kuo's daring fiction collection comprising the novel and other related stories of China. Here is an important new work, revisiting the China that led to the student uprising in 1989, and poses the larger question of what China will become as the balance of power in the world totters and shifts. As always, Kuo manages to sneak his way through history, this time via* qiàopài *(bridge) tournaments that Ge competes in as Deng's partner. The narrative becomes a contemplation of yet another turbulent Chinese moment, one best expressed by a line in the poem Ge pens,* But I feel as if I'm walking in circles. *Ge's story is fascinating, this fictional witness to the grand moments of Chinese history, one who records, verbatim, all the meetings he is privileged to attend. This dark comedy is both history lesson and an unpacking of modern China through the "fragility of words on words," this country kissed by Mao to awaken for its rise in the 21st Century. Absolutely a must-read for our global times.*

—Xu Xi, novelist, editor, and essayist
Hong Kong Rose, Habit of a Foreign Sky, City Voices

Other Books by Alex Kuo

The Window Tree	1971, poetry
New Letters from Hiroshima	1974, poetry
Changing the River	1986, poetry
Chinese Opera	1998, novel
This Fierce Geography	1999, poetry
Lipstick and Other Stories	2001, fiction
Panda Diaries	2006, novel
White Jade and Other Stories	2008, fiction
A Chinaman's Chance	2011, poetry
The Man who Dammed the Yangtze	2011, novel
My Private China	2013, non-fiction
shanghai.shanghai.shanghai	2015, novel (four editions)
Meeting Words at the Gate	2015, poetry (bi-lingual)

REDBAT BOOKS
PACIFIC NORTHWEST
WRITERS SERIES

MAO'S KISSES

A Novel of June 4, 1989

by Alex Kuo

redbat
books

redbat books
2019

Printed in the United States of America

First Edition: June 4, 2019

Trade Paperback ISBN 978-1-946970-93-0
Hardcover with Dust Jacket ISBN 978-1-946970-89-3

Library of Congress Control Number: 2019939918

Published by
redbat books
La Grande, OR 97850
www.redbatbooks.com

Text set in Garamond Premier Pro

Book design by
Kristin Summers, redbat design | www.redbatdesign.com

For Zoe Filipkowska,
for the half century of our projects, my love

Our ability to murder each other grows stronger every day, and the new ways of mutual massacre that we have devised are almost as ingenious as the new devises that we have discovered for writing poetry.
— LAO SHE, *Cat Country*, WILLIAM LYELL, translator

China was to become a nation of perpetual chaos, of ceaseless political upheavals and revolutionary uprisings.
— Z.Y. KUO, *Confessions of a Chinese Scientist*

With the potential troublemakers visible and active, the crackdown that inevitably followed eliminated them.
— MASHA GESSEN, *The Future Is History*

With an early October morning's breeze flipping up the lower flap of his military trench coat, Chairman Mao went to Beijing's bus depot and scrawled his name on the dust of the hoods of the five buses still working after the civil war ended in 1949. He then stepped back and carefully blew off the dust on his hand, wafting soft kisses from its finger tips. This magnanimity did not change; it only magnified, beginning that early afternoon when he stood atop the Gate of Heavenly Peace in Tiananmen Square as yet another Middle Kingdom emperor, and smiling and waving kisses to the Pathé News cameras, he proclaimed the establishment of the People's Republic of China. After a protracted revolution half a century in the making, he moved into an upscale home with swimming pool inside the secure Zhongnanhai compound just west of the Three Lakes [*Editor's fact check: bad translation. It should be Three Seas.*] in central Beijing, where for most of the next quarter century, as both the Chairman of the Chinese Communist Party and later the nation's first president, he concocted plans for one Great Leap Forward after another with devastating consequences.

In his notebook Ge tracked Mao's first official act as China's paramount leader: he salvaged the deficient Beijing Municipal Bus Company left with seventy-six broken down buses at the end of the war, with only five still working on October 1. Nobody knew what happened to America's 15,000 Lend-Leased Dodge T-234 trucks, but the ever-imperial Mao was to change all that with his right palm open and slightly raised so he could blow a breath of fresh, sparking smackos to those clutching the right party membership in the next five months: seventy-six *Ikaruses* from Hungary, and fifty-two advanced Skodas from Czechoslovakia that could cruise at 60 kph with fifty passengers.

Then there was Mao's kiss. What was it? What did it mean? A shower of affection? A familial greeting? A farewell to Generalissimo Chiang Kai-shek and the Kuomintang as they set sail for Formosa? A goodbye before a public self-criticism session, or a beheading outside the south entrance to the Palace? Or Chairman Mao's gift to Premier Zhou Enlai for his well-placed phone calls to protect such people as Deng Xiaoping, Lao She and Madame Sun in 1966 and 1967 from being savaged by the violence of the Red Guards that Mao had mobilized in the Great Proletariat Cultural Revolution? Certainly more appealing than the gift to the world of his embalmed body on display inside a crystal coffin in the mausoleum in the heart of the capital, a national heirloom as tourist attraction for both domestic as well as foreign visitors to Beijing, second in popularity to the Forbidden Palace and way above the distant third, the Great Wall at Badaling.

The further Ge moved into the shadows of Zhongnanhai's central archives in early 1989 forty years later, the more he became cautious about excavating material and copying it into his notebook for the novel about the Cultural Revolution he's thinking about writing before its memory disappeared entirely from the collective amnesia of the nation's history. Already the word from the top had announced that the nation was severely fatigued by too much talk about it, time to move on. A project for a rainy day in the future, as the Americans would say, Ge thought, just in case he lost his job and its security clearance hanging around his neck. And get it published in Hong Kong, or Berlin.

Already his birth name of G had been challenged during the extensive vetting interrogations for his high level appointment within the central government, the personal notetaker for the preeminent leader Deng Xiaoping and his main partner in the game of *qiáopái*. He explained that his parents who taught novels at Beida had named him after a crazy, shape-changing fictional character by a Czech writer, but his interlocutors insisted on changing it since the word in Chinese meant a mental derangement that would foment turmoil and dissolve the social glue of the nation. His job description demanded someone who could be trusted to be truthful, discreet and normal, someone who would not do anything to alter or rearrange his identity. It didn't matter when G pointed out that *crazy* has other meanings too, such as someone who is daring and innovative and indeed, there's at least one crazy dog on every block in the university district in western Beijing that's named after its progenitor, Kafka, he added. No matter, they threatened. He had to change his name to Ge, they insisted again. Just an addition of an inconsequential radical to your name won't change who you are, his interlocutors promised, just one silent vowel. Or else.

The more he deliberated over this novel he's thinking about writing, the more he felt he's already in a book someone else was writing.

15

2.

That night Ge transferred his notes onto his computer, but they didn't look right on the monitor. The words looked like random flecks of carbon of no importance to anyone except maybe a cultural anthropologist. And it didn't take him long to finally face the dread of admitting that he had no interest in writing historical fiction, or Mao, if he was seventy percent correct, and who is to decide what falls into the seventy and what into the thirty.

So, delete and dump.

Delete and dump.

Delete and dump.

Then deep into the night he started writing an account in the first person about a couple of young California missionaries who had set up a free language learning table next to his letter-writing stall, at his place of work in the busy Panjiayuan Flea Market just southeast of Tiananmen Square.

> *A week ago two young Americans in their early twenties appeared and squeezed a display table next to my small folding table and short wooden stools. With their wide smiles, they introduced themselves as Ginny and William, English language teachers representing Pasadena's Educational Services Exchange with China and assured me that they would not disrupt what I was doing. The man wore a narrow, dark tie and clean and ironed white shirt ev-*

ery day, and the woman different skirts with floral prints, definitely not the torn jeans and rumpled jackets associated with American experts on teaching appointments in the university district. But underneath her smile, Ginny appeared to be looking around too carefully to be a fundamentalist believer, as if she's trying to find something else to do in Beijing that would be more satisfying.

Their heavy rucksacks contained multiple copies of pamphlets for their learning programs, as well as language cassette tapes and small New Testament bibles with green vinyl-covers, all for free, they promised in Mandarin with a loud and severe southern accent. They also assured me that while they were interdenominational Christians, they were not in China to proselytize and convert, and smiled again.

On his way to the market the next morning, Ge stepped into his small kitchen area where he kept his computer and printer on his large kitchen and work table stacked with probability books and novels in both English and Chinese. There he stared in horror at what he had written the night before. Nothing here either, a stagnant social realism that did not disturb the anesthetized culture of ideas and memories that were walled-in brick by brick in this China, real or imagined.

He added some extra envelopes, writing paper, and postage stamps to his book bag just in case, found his key to his bicycle lock, clipped on the right legging fastener, and bounded down the stairway two steps at a time in order to get to work past the Fourth Ring Road under construction just before the market opened at 8:30. He did not want to disappoint.

3.

And just in case was right. A line of migrant workers had already formed before Ge moved his small folding table and smaller stools from the locker to his rented stall.

They were mostly middle-aged men from distant interior rural provinces. Clustered in groups of two or three, they were attempting to exchange information and help each other find work, food and shelter in this Beijing modernizing at a furious pace. Unschooled, they could not read or write and did not speak the same dialect, even though the Mandarin-based Pŭtōnghuà had been declared China's official language first in 1932 by the Republic of China, and later inserted as Article 19 into the national Constitution at a meeting of the People's Republic of China at its Fifth National People's Congress in 1982.

Even after several decades of this national mandate, away from the learning opportunities of an urban environment they could barely greet each other in a common oral language and communicated mostly by gesturing, repeating, repeating louder, and pointing. Two consecutive years of flooding and drought had demolished the production of the already failing collective agricultural farms and, attempting to avoid the famines resulting from the Great Leap Forward that caused more than fifty million deaths in the fifties, including Ge's sister, these men resisted hanging about the village with no work in sight and migrated to urban centers by the thousands and to Beijing at 15,000 daily in the last few months. One less mouth to feed. By foot and hitched on draught-drawn hog or chicken carts, rural poverty became urban homelessness overnight.

Clothed in tatters, they arrived with no work skills and were exploited as construction workers in this capital of China's preeminent leader Deng Xiaoping's modernizing Beijing, mostly moving building materials and debris balanced on twin shoulder baskets from dawn to dusk. They did not even qualify for street sweeping jobs that were reserved for those with party connections, and somehow survived like the rickshaw boys of the twenties and thirties in cities like Shanghai and Hong Kong. They quickly learned that newspapers and cardboard were the most helpful survival materials, helping each other in finding food and clothing for the severe Beijing winter, and locating some place warm to sleep where they would not be evicted or beaten.

Most of them found some way to let their families know that they were alive, a few of them finding letter-writers who would attempt to understand their regional dialects, transcribe their messages, provide the proper postage and charge a small fee. But not Ge, who did it for free, even the postage. He wanted to do something helpful for someone in need. And besides, he made enough money in his salaried government appointment, and as a card player, especially in the game of *qiáopái*, for which his generous patron was Deng Xiaoping. Ge was his partner for competitions at national and regional tournaments, institutional competitions, as well as for invited games on Sunday afternoons and evenings at his home. A black Audi with special license plates usually picked up Ge just before one to take him to these games at Deng's home on Mei Langgu Street, just a short ten-minute drive to Zhongnanhai where almost all of the highest-level government officials and party cadres and their families lived.

4.

The first time G met Deng Xiaoping took place at a *qiáopái* table some twenty-five years ago [*Editor's fact check: it was twenty-three years ago, just four months before the start of the Great Proletariat Cultural Revolution in May, 1966.*] at the annual Class A Jilin Provincial championships. After seventeen rounds of competition between thirty seeded and twenty-four unseeded teams, the championship round between G's team (Chess Academy of Jilin Province) and Deng's team (Beijing No. 2 Ball Bearing Works) took place in Ballrooms A and B of the Shangri-La Hotel on the morning of the seventh and final day of the tournament.

Deng looked well rested at the end of the week of intensive competition. As the General Secretary of the party, the vice premier and one of the five members of the important Standing Committee of the Politburo, he had brought his team—eight players, a dozen substitutes and practice surrogates, two coaches, a non-playing captain and Deng's personal assistant Wang Ruilin—on a specially requisitioned train fourteen hours from Beijing to Changchun, north of North Korea, and stayed and dined at the walled enclave built by the Japanese during its occupation. Famous throughout China for its stewed venison dinners that originated with the Tungusic-speaking tribal Oroqens in the Greater Khingnan Mountains to the north, this secluded resort at the northwest edge of the city had become one of the two most favored and exclusive vacation destinations for the top party apparatchiks, the other being Hainan Island where the women's national *qiáopái* teams trained every other year before major international matches such as the Venice Cup or the World Women's Pairs held every four years.

Throughout the morning half of the match, Deng was quiet, totally absorbed in the game and did not engage in any meaningless chitchat with his partner or opponents. He sorted, arranged and played his cards smoothly, and carefully wrote his bids with his own scoring pen on the small square of paper before sliding it under the diagonal screen [*Editor's note: the northwest to southeast screen was designed to prevent cheating partners from sending visual signals to each other.*] to the player on his left, and played each card identically in an even tempo. Even though every player and the directors of the game knew who he was, he was treated as if he was just another *qiáopái* player, no favors in the play or rule suspension in the case of a minor rule violation.

And in turn Deng reciprocated this same courtesy to all the other players, even to the head director, who spoke and acted so Han Chinese that G thought he must have been at least half Korean. But it was evident to G that Deng kept a careful eye on everything in the room, even little things away from their table, the individual staff members emptying the ashtrays and filling the water cups, the reporters gathered in groups in the lobby and looking at the competition on giant Japanese monitors, the efficient caddies moving the eight card trays to be played in duplicate by the other half of the teams in the adjoining Ballroom B. He didn't miss a thing.

Not bad, G thought, for someone with a western Sichuan accent and a thirty-year veteran [*Editor's fact check: twenty-nine year veteran, as Deng joined the march in January of 1937.*] of the Long March, alert and choosing all the right lines of play for the provincial championship's final round of sixty-four hands, with an outside temperature of minus seventeen Celsius this January morning.

At the morning break after the first sixteen hands the score was close with Deng's Beijing No. 2 Ball Bearing ahead by an insignificant eleven IMPs before its non-playing captain, noticing his pair in Ballroom B had flamed out from the intensity, substituted a fresh pair. At the lunch break halfway through the match, G's Chess Academy had caught up a few points but still trailed by an insignificant five IMPs.

The afternoon session started with the players making the mandated ballroom seating changes so that the morning's opponents would not be duplicated. As the Chess Academy only qualified four players for this tournament, the team stayed the same for the afternoon half as it had all week. The No. 2 Ball Bearing non-playing captain substituted yet a third pair to play the last thirty-two hands against G and his partner. At the afternoon break, the score was even closer between the two teams with Ball Bearing still leading, this time by just one IMP. The two teams were quite even up to this point. Anything could happen with sixteen hands left to play. There can be as much as a twelve point swing on any one hand, even at this level of play: a wrong count of an opponent's card distribution because of his partner's false carding, a misunderstood redouble, taking a finesse on a guess instead of working out an end play.

And it all came down to one hand, Board 31 in which G and his partner, perhaps dulled by the drudgery of some sixty hands that day bid aggressively to seven spades on this hand, G being south.

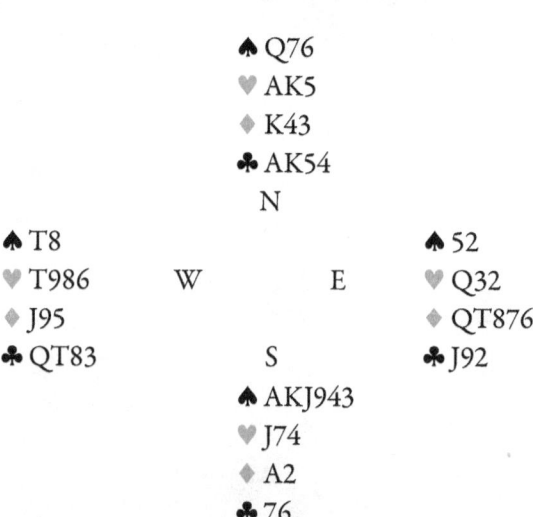

The bidding was straight forward. G as the dealer South scribbled 1S on the piece of bidding paper and passed it to his left, and it came back from his right a moment later with his partner bidding 4NT and asking for aces, eventually ending in the Grand Slam of seven spades, with the opening lead of ♥T. G won the first trick with dummy's ♠A, played two rounds of spades to draw the outside four trumps, then won two club tricks before trumping a third round of clubs in his hand. Next he won with ♥K before winning two more spade tricks, leaving this position.

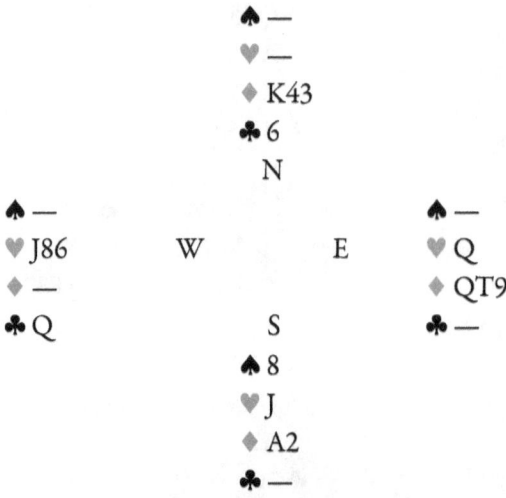

G played the ♠8 next, and both his opponents were caught in a double squeeze, allowing G to make his contract, which turned out to be the play that won the championship for the Chess Academy of Jilin Province with the following final standings for the top six teams.

1. Chess Academy of Jilin Province
2. Beijing No. 2 Ball Bearing Works
3. Jilin University
4. Jilin Oil Field
5. First Automobile Factory
6. Second Aeronautical Engineering Institute

At the concluding award ceremony, Deng Xiaoping went up to G and congratulated him on his daring bidding and executing the double squeeze to win the match. Deng and his teammate ended up in six spades, making only six, while G bid seven in Ballroom B and made seven for a thirteen IMPs swing. Sixty-four hands down to just one that made the difference.

—My teammates said you made seven on a beautiful double squeeze against them on Board 31, good play, good play all morning when I was at your table. Mr. Technician.

—I cannot detect any accent in your Pūtōnghuà, he added, not like mine, full of Sichuan. You must be from Beijing, no? he asked just before leaving the hotel with his team.

A moment later Deng's personal assistant Wang Ruilin returned and asked G for his Beijing contact information. Comrade Deng would like to meet you in Beijing, he explained.

5.

G's meeting with Comrade Deng did not happen after he returned to Beijing from the tournament in Changchun. In fact it did not happen for another ten years, as 1966 turned out to be a very bad year for Deng.

Convinced that China was opening up too rapidly and moving away from the dictatorship of the proletariat, Chairman Mao initiated the Great Proletariat Cultural Revolution and mobilized the Red Guards in May. Adding his wife the actress Jiang Qing, Wang Hongwen, Yao Wenyuan and Zhang Chenqiao, they become the Gang of Five and initiated a period of rampant and indiscriminate violence throughout the country for almost ten years.

A wave of bloodletting and vindictive torture and murder took place in Beijing in August of that first year, where thousands were killed or pushed to suicide, where intellectuals, professionals, artists, musicians, teachers, Muslims, and especially novelists were targeted.

Deng was not immune from this onslaught. In fact, he had been called out as a *capitalist roader* and *counterrevolutionary* and publicly criticized as a bourgeoisie for playing the game of *qiáopái*. His appropriation of state trains to take his *qiáopái* team to tournaments across the country was seen as evidence that he was criminally corrupt as well.

Fortunately in early October three years later, Chairman Mao decided to provide some protection for this exceptionally talented administrator by placing him and his wife Zhou Lin under house arrest in the Zhongnanhai compound where

the Red Guards could not touch him. But his eldest son Pu-
fang was not so lucky: he was tortured and then pushed out
of a fourth-story window in a downtown Beijing building, his
two broken legs confining him to a wheelchair for the rest of
his life.

Then in early October three years later, Deng and Zhou
Lin and his stepmother Xia Bogen were flown in an unmarked
People's Liberation Army plane to the small city of Nancheng
in southern Jiangxi Province for ideological rehabilitation,
re-education in Mao Zedong Thought, self-criticism for his
liberal thinking, and physical labor for both of them at a tractor repair shop. Wanting to protect them and keep them out
of the reach of the ferocious local Red Guards in this isolat-
ed and conservative, rural environment, Premier Zhou Enlai
made a phone call to the local party officials in Nanchang to
make sure that the Dengs would be housed comfortably and
protected in the PLA's military barracks in Nancheng for the
next four years.

6.

In order to maintain a positive outlook on their future, the Dengs pulled their lives together very quickly with some kind of daily routine so that they could devote more time to doing what they enjoyed. But they would have to begin each day after breakfast with an hour of supervised reading from Mao Zedong Thought books before going to work. Six days a week they took the short one-kilometer walk to the tractor repair shop on a route that was patrolled to keep away any trouble, and in the evenings they listened to their radios. They also read to each other from the books they were able to bring with them, a novel from the Song era and one from the Qing, *Dream of the Red Chamber, Water Margin*, and several novels from Russian and French in translation.

Every day after lunch Deng would walk on a garden path around the house forty times, always thinking about what he would do when Mao would at last acknowledge that he had criticized himself enough to be called back to Beijing, as he suspected he would be. After all, he had not been dumped and trashed altogether or made to disappear. Occasionally he would write articles on what he had thought about on these daily walks, with detailed notes on his priorities for modernizing China, with emphasis on improving agricultural and industrial production, science and technology development and, most importantly, securing national stability before any of the other three could take place.

Once every two or three months he would write a respectful and solicitous letter to the paramount leader Chairman Mao and let the cat out of the bag, a reminder that he was ready to work again to serve the people and the country, with specific suggestions on how the economy could be stimulated. Preferring the use of aphorisms over the language of abstract ideology, he wrote *No matter if the cat is black or white as long as it catches the mouse* in one of them. At the same time, Beijing residents showed their support of Deng by hanging small bottles from trees and placing them in the windows of their homes in the hutongs, as his name in Chinese meant Little Bottle.

They would listen to the news every night at 10 P.M. from Central People's Radio and when the atmospheric reception allowed they would stretch the antennae of their shortwave radio the entire length of their living area, and then the three of them would huddle together with their tea and listen to the news from outside China, Deng paying particular attention in 1972 to the international reports on the chess Match of the Century in Reykjavik, Iceland, between the young and temperamental American Bobby Fischer and the Soviet Boris Spassky, as well as reports about the international competition in the game of *qiáopái* in which both the Italian Blue Team and the Italian Women's Team won their events at the Bridge Olympiad held at Miami Beach, Florida. One follow up broadcast, sponsored by the American publication *Sports Illustrated* and Coca-Cola, made a commentary on the Italian Blue Team as well as the British great Terence Reese cheating at international *qiáopái* competitions.

—Fischer is a genius, Deng told his wife Zhou Lin after one of these broadcasts one night, and he will win, if he can keep his emotions under control and actually complete the match scheduled for two months.

And on another night he said, I have never understood why the Italians and Reese have to cheat. They are the best players in the world. Belladonna and Giorgio have this super-precision bidding convention, and Reese and his partner Shapiro have this sophisticated discarding system. All legal. The Italians have won sixteen world titles in eighteen years; they don't need to cheat by tapping their partner's shoe under the table to send signals. And Reese had won every major *qiáopái* title in the world; he and Shapiro do not have to hold their cards in such a way that the front fingers show the number of hearts they have. If they can't figure that heart count legally, they aren't even good enough to play in my kitchen.

—No, no, no, Zhou corrected Deng, even though she didn't play the game. But she was a good listener and Deng was beginning to have hearing problems from his degenerative nerve disease and tinnitus, especially his right ear. They didn't say Belladonna and Giogio cheated, she said louder this second time. They were Facchini and Zucchelli, and this was after the Blue Team had retired.

On his walk forty times around the house the next afternoon, he thought about writing a book on cheating in *qiáopái*, just as Reese and Shapiro had claimed they were going to write a book too and had experimented with their cheating as a case study just to see what would happen. Just as he turned at the last corner on the garden path, it struck him, a bourgeoisie outcast under supervised house arrest in Nancheng, if he would ever play *qiáopái* again. Silence.

That evening he skipped dinner, went to bed without a book, and did not listen to the news on either Central People's Radio, Voice of America, or British Broadcasting Corporation.

7.

In early 1973, Premier Zhou Enlai convinced the paramount leader Chairman Mao that Deng had been exiled from Beijing long enough: letters of self-criticisms and his extensive political rehabilitation in addition to four years of working in the tractor factory, mopping floors, helping out with his stepmother's small vegetable garden and chickens, and splitting wood for cooking and heating, led him to believe that Deng was ready to be brought back to the capital. His talents and experience in providing the administrative and organizational leadership for the country was desperately needed.

In the next seventeen years, Deng did just that, and he continued to play *qiáopái* at a few tournaments within driving distance, as well as inviting friends to his home on Mei Langgu Street for dinner and then *qiáopái* once or twice a week depending on his schedule.

But first Deng kept his promise made to G in 1966 at the end of the Jilin Provincial championship in Changchun. They met in Deng's modest home less than ten minutes from Zhongnanhai, where most of his important meetings took place and well secured by the armed guards of the Central Security Bureau's Unit 8341.

—Thank you for coming, Deng started the meeting.

—It has been almost ten years since our *qiáopái* competition in Changchun.

—That is so, no matter, Deng interrupted. First I want to ask if you would like to be my *qiáopái* partner. No lessons; I learn by observing and memorizing hands when it's useful.

Stunned, G did not know what to say.

—And also my personal notetaker, some very important meetings.

G was curious and asked about it.

—Yes, yes, but tape recordings have problems when they are transcribed, often unintentional mistakes made by the typist unfamiliar with the accent of the speaker, and sometimes intentionally for political fealty, real or imagined. And they can be erased, like the American President Nixon did in Washington earlier this year.

—You know the verbatim transcription of notes you take down of what people say in a meeting, Deng continued, they will be remembered and read quite differently in the future by these same people who will deny that they said them. So be very, very careful of your handwriting; it may not be recording the truth. I know. I was a notetaker at the beginning of the Long March in 1937 in Zuyni where I was also putting out the propaganda sheet Red Star.

But nevertheless he wanted someone he could trust, Deng explained, like what he had read in American history about James Madison taking notes for Thomas Jefferson at the Philadelphia Constitutional Convention in 1787 that lasted almost four months. Deng had also examined the published record of all the four hundred-and-forty-eight *qiáopái* hands that G played in Changchun that week, and came to the conclusion that his bidding was remarkably reflective of what he was actually holding, when possible. [*Editor's note, tweeted from Gianarrigo Rone, president of the World Bridge Federation: except for one in which G totally distorted his hand and wrote down a forcing bid by naming a suit he had a void in, before making the final bid of six diamonds that could not have been arrived at safely in any other way.*]

—You are very precise and accurate; you can be trusted, not like most of the other players in this town. For many of these meetings for you to take notes, I won't even be there, as I can't hear what people are saying. But I can hear enough with my left ear to know your Pǔtōnghuà is much better than most people's in this town, even when it originated here.

He said that he had admired G's ability to keep that neutral distance at the *qiáopái* table and not be overwhelmed by the deluge of his opponents' chitchat, seemingly just out of touch enough to be able to judge people accurately, remember them, and continue the game.

—I want you to treat our meetings in the same way, but also to record in the margin what you think the people are really saying. A slight wink of an eye or wagging a finger can entirely change the meaning of a word. And as for metaphors, hesitations, and ironies, you're entirely on your own. Sometimes they are very simple and often stupid, as in the KISS [*Editor's note: Keep It Simple Stupid.*] bidding system in qiáopái, as you know, or at the other end it can be very convoluted like the Kraków Club that only Polish number theory mathematicians understand it.

At this point G thought perhaps it would be easier to get at the event's truth by writing fiction, instead of reporting, even with photographs, which can always lie and distort. And in his memory of the same hands from Changchun that Deng used for this interview, G knew that as a *qiáopái* player with an ethnic Hakka connection, and being the shortest person in the room most of the time, Deng was the realist who played the hand that he was dealt, rather than one imagined.

—And just one more thing. For state stability and security reasons, you will be vetted extensively by the Ministry of State Security. Be patient with some of those polite administrative thugs: you might be asked to change your name. But you can say you play *qiáopái*, in English or Pǔtōnghuà, it's okay now.

8.

One fall morning five years later, Ge was summoned to a nine o'clock meeting in Deng's home office. He was used to seeing the huge stacks of papers colliding and skidding into each other on the top of Deng's desk before some of them had to be picked up from the floor. Fifteen daily papers, plus translations from the foreign press, folders of reports from the provincial party secretaries, internal memoranda collected by the Xinhua News Agency, summaries of major national and provincial activities provided by the party Secretariat, drafts of documents from the agencies in Zhongnanhai that needed his comments, and completed directives that needed his signature and stamp. Ge also knew that Deng would sabotage the daily attempts by his office director Chen Yun and personal assistant Wang Ruilin to lessen his reading time by their pre-selecting only five newspapers: he wanted to personally decide what to read and what not to. And it was rumored that everything would be read and returned to be filed at five each afternoon, at the latest.

—It's done, Deng announced to Ge, as you know already, since you were taking notes at some of those meetings. We have worked out all the details with Brzezinski and Woodcock, good union man, agreement on full normalization between us and the Americans, including removing all their military personnel from Taiwan within a year. [*Editor's fact check: at the time Leonard Woodcock was the director of the American Liaison Office in Beijing, he had a staff of about thirty; there are now more than a thousand officers assigned to the*

Embassy in Beijing surrounded by CCTV and guarded by the U.S. Marines.]

President Jimmy Carter had invited the preeminent leader Deng [*Editor's note: Vice-Premier and Chairman of the Central Military Commission of the Communist Party of China were Deng's highest official titles, and he avoided the personality cult of displaying portraits of him in any government building throughout the country when he was in office.*] and his wife Zhou for a nine-day visit to the United States.

—I would like you and interpreter Tang Wensheng to come with us in January, Deng asked. She was born in Brooklyn, and had translated for Chairman Mao and Premier Zhou's meetings with President Nixon and Kissinger, and at the United Nations.

Ge's meeting with Tang that afternoon lasted well past the security guards changing shifts at the house at five. They started by discussing their anticipated duties in Washington, which later included Philadelphia, Atlanta, Houston, Seattle, and New York, their seating arrangement with the presence of American interpreters and the security detail from both countries, in formal settings such as a White House dinner as well as the informal scrum of a Texas rodeo.

—You know Mr. Ge, hmm. Sorry, too used to that formality. I learned Chinese only when my parents moved to Beijing after the Korean War was over, hmm, she hesitated. I learned very early that when I have learned a new language, most of my memories stayed behind. Pǔtōnghuà is not an easy language to learn. Hmm, for its delicate pronunciation I watched *The Sound of Music* dubbed in Pǔtōnghua and listened to Peking Opera and that woman with the perfect Beijing accent announcing the morning temperatures on Radio Beijing, from *Beijing* to *Caracas* to *Ulaanbaatar* to *Puyallup*.

—But it mattered little, Tang continued, nudging up her wire-framed glasses. Chairman Mao came from a southern province. Those hot peppers kept him from the nuances and delicacies of the Beijing dialect; and Premier Zhou's Pǔtōnghua is not very good either, born into the rural, northern, wu-speaking Jiangxu Province. He is better in French or English.

Nodding agreement, Ge started fidgeting with the alphabet in his head. Ever since he studied number theory at the university, he would use this mental segue from a boring conversation. It usually started with a sequence of prime numbers, but in deference to Tang's company, it began this time with the first letter in the Chinese dictionary, the imperative, horizontal semantic radical, trailed by a long line of fractals to the left, trying to mimic a dotted line all the way to $\log^{\circ}\sin\frac{1}{2}$. When that sequence evaporated, Ge continued this linguistic exercise in English with the first letter in the alphabet, *A*, then *B*, then *C*, on down the line until he stopped at *T*, the three *T*s, Tibet, Taiwan, and Tiananmen, until they were all gone—disappeared from the national language translated or not—even all the service curlicues and deadweight articles whose function was to grace the idiom and which only confuse a foreigner learning English for the first time: *the*, *an*, and *a*. He was convinced that state censorship always began with the word, he continued thinking while looking straight at the distinguished Tang with the power resume who was rumored to have interrupted America's Secretary of State Henry Kissinger while she was interpreting for Premier Zhou. Are we talking history here, or is language just metaphors and symbols which can't be trusted and can be fatal when they are repeated enough to morph into clichés?

—You know, Mr. Ge, Tang continued using this formal address, some of Comrade Deng's other interpreters insist on an advance text for their work, but I don't think he works that way. He's not going to have this text for us. We'll have to punt, as they say in Brooklyn.

9.

In its January 1 issue, *Time* magazine announced the selection of Deng Xiaoping as Man of the Year, and on its cover printed his portrait over the backdrop of a Sung Dynasty painting of a well-regulated mountain landscape.

Four weeks later Deng boarded a People's Liberation Army-piloted Boeing 707 in Beijing for a fourteen-hour flight to Andrews Air Force Base near Washington, becoming the first Chinese leader to visit the United States. For much of the flight, Deng stayed awake and sat by himself near a window thinking about what he would say publicly, occasionally looking at the prepared notes for two speeches, which he would later abandon, much to the consternation of his interpreter Tang. Occasionally he would nod and look down the aisle at Tang and Ge sitting next to each other, and then at the thirty-some Chinese reporters behind them. It had been previously agreed that Vietnam, civil rights, continuing American arms sales to Taiwan would not come up for discussion. But how would he react to the anticipated protest by the American left that have accused him of betraying Mao's revolution, or what if the evangelical Christian or pro-Taiwan demonstrations got out of control, as well as how to respond to off-the-record questions from the more aggressive TV anchors?

Away from the main cabin, Ge was wondering if the American Secret Service would actually enforce the requirement for photojournalists to remove the lens from their Speed Graphic cameras and fire a flash before they would be allowed into the same room as Deng, as previously agreed to. Revolutions and counter-revolutions in China's twentieth century, like imagined numbers they came up in Ge's half-sleep on this long flight, starting with the anti-imperial Boxer Rebellion at the beginning of the century, then 1911, 1919, 1928, 1935, and the long one that started in 1966, each one of these years affixing itself as a number onto the six sides of a perpetually rolling die. Maybe stability is just an illusion that a big-character revolutionary poster hanging in Tiananmen Square can destroy overnight. The dream ended with the question, Will the real China stand up?

10.

At the elegant White House state banquet, Deng Xiaoping was seated between President Carter and the actress Shirley MacLaine, with Tang and the president's interpreter behind them and Ge off to the side, taking notes.

After the introductory toasts, President Carter asked Vice-Premier about his thoughts on the achievements of American missionaries in China.

—You know, when I was very young, I used to contribute the nickels I had saved up to support the Baptists' missionaries in China. What are your thoughts about letting these missionaries come to China again?

At this point Ge noticed that interpreter Tang seemed to be getting a bit anxious over this conversation.

—Some of them were very good people, they set up many schools and hospitals, President Carter said, saving the moment.

Ge wrote a note in the margin of his notebook to look up the Southern Baptist missionaries' activities in China.

—Well yes, Deng conceded with a smile, perhaps that was a good thing, except too many of them tried to change our way of life, change our children's names and steal our babies and furniture. At this time we are not ready for that again.

President Carter then turned to Shirley MacLaine.

—You know that she has just returned from a visit to your country with several of her women friends. She wrote and produced a documentary that has been reviewed as presenting a very positive image of a progressive China.

[*Editor's fact check: MacLaine's documentary,* The Other Half of the Sky: A China Memoir, *was nominated in 1975 for an Oscar as a feature documentary. Produced with the close supervision of China's State Administration of Press, Publications, Radio, Film and Television, the seventy-four minute film of scripted interviews with officials and citizens presented an utopian China with gender equality between men and women, and that there was no corruption, hunger, poverty, crime, despair, unhappiness, racism, or AIDS.*]

—Yes, and I met a professor in Beijing, just a wonderful, wonderful man, MacLaine said. He told me on camera how much he was grateful for what he had learned about life because he had been sent to the countryside for physical labor and raised tomatoes during the Cultural Revolution. Such a wise man, she added.

Ge noticed that sitting behind the peanut farmer president, Tang was humming and hesitating a lot while interpreting this conversation that she was translating for Deng, but she did manage to finish it accurately, at which point Deng turned to look at her before replying.

—He was lying, he said and turned to look at President Carter's interpreter to make sure he got this right before continuing. Professors should be teaching classes and not planting vegetables.

In Beijing almost exactly ten years later, with Deng Xiaoping firmly established as the preeminent leader of China with only the titles of Vice-Premier and Chairman of the Central Military Commission, the American missionaries were back, not the Jesuits or nuns of the Immaculate Conception, or Methodists or Presbyterians, those that built schools and hospitals in addition to churches; now they were the evangelical, fundamentalist Christians who called themselves non-denominational or inter-denominational, or Southern Baptists or Missouri Synod Lutherans hiding under this umbrella, or certified English language teachers with Oral Roberts University in Tulsa, Oklahoma, or pitched in the stall next to Ge's like Ginny and William with the Educational Services Exchange with China headquartered in Pasadena, California.

This morning a man with a stooped back who stood first in line at Ge's letter writing stall had a heavy southern accent, but he managed to convince Ge to write his letter to his wife with brush and ink instead of pencil or ball-point pen. This unusual request surprised Ge, facing an itinerant migrant worker homeless in Beijing but familiar enough with the different writing instruments to indicate a preference for the traditional.

—Today I pay with Mao talisman, he promised, bringing out a crumpled color photograph of paramount leader Chairman Mao attached to a decorative red tassel.

—No matter, you keep. All free today, Ge insisted while he brought out the bottled ink and bamboo brush from deep inside his bag. Ge's not going to accept a true believer giving up his Mao talisman, his only link to any luck in his life. And besides, what will Ge do with it? Hang it from the rearview mirror of his car like every other cab driver in down, to stave off accidents and evil spirits from a car he doesn't have?

Then they spent a few moments chatting quietly together while Ge familiarized himself with his client's voice and accent before settling down to transcribe his letter to his wife, pausing several times to get both the personal idiom and southern dialect right.

> *My Dear Wife,*
>
> *For far too long I have left you for another chance. This city is so remote and I feel alien in a strange land. The bitter winter is past and the howling winds from the north is almost gone, I am not so sure. But I am all right just now. So stop your worries for me who has implicated you in my misery.*
>
> *Yesterday I received your letter carried by our friend. When he read it to me I could not keep tears from running down my cheeks thinking about the sufferings of our life and our painful separation.*
>
> *The only thing that sustains me* [Editor's note: here the English language is inadequate for the task of an accurate translation of this letter.] *here is looking for work and hoping I am not cheated when I find it. Most days I stand trapped in long line and find no work. I earn very little money to send more than two paper wu jiao to you this week.*
>
> *I pray this letter will reach you and give you with some consolation.*
>
> *Your unfortunate husband*

Ge licked the stamp and when Unfortunate Husband wasn't looking, tucked a purple five yuan note into the envelope before sealing it with a paste brush. The letter was addressed to the reliable green China Post office in Laomiao Village just outside Nancheng in southern Jiangxi Province.

12.

In his apartment that evening, Ge looked at the paper currency he had set aside for his card games. The notes were carefully bundled and banded together by their colors. He noted the venerable helmsman Chairman Mao continuing to occupy the nation's collective memory on every denominational yuan note, or at least his image, even twenty-three years after his death. One yuan on light green, five on purple, ten on blue, twenty on brown, fifty on deep green and one hundred on red. [*Editor's fact check: There had also been four other yuan bills picturing Han couples masquerading in indigenous costumes instead of Mao's image, but they went out of circulation in the early eighties: one yuan in magenta, two in green, five in brown, and ten in blue.*]

The calamitous earthquakes along the twenty-five mile-long Tangshan Fault of 7.8 and 7.1 on the RMS in 1976 that took more than sixty-five thousand lives, foreshadowed one more in fewer than six weeks with that of Chairman Mao's third heart attack in four months, his death five days later signifying a dynastic ending in the old calendar.

And within a month, the remaining four of the Gang of Five were cuffed by the CSB's Unit 8341 and charged with treason and responsibility for initiating a decade of terror that took more than thirty-five thousand lives, many of them indigenous Muslim minorities in Mongolia.

Ge looked at these numbers with increasing skepticism about the centuries long Han domination of his nation and both its individual and systemic racism against its indigenous peoples, the Miaos to the south, the Oroqens to the north, the Uyĝhurs to the west, those surviving groups in the mountains of Han-occupied Taiwan to the east, and that's not including the Tibetans and the Mongolians.

During the period of reforming the nation's *bad elements* programs, Ge's parents were sent to the Re-Education through Labor camp at the southern Guizhou Province. Living in a dormitory in a small rural border town and assigned to the terraced rice farms developed by the Miaos, they spent four years learning to accept and respect the warmth and friendship extended to them by members of the largest remaining community of Miaos and Hmongs in China who had not escaped to Vietnam, even after a series of rebellions, including one in 1911 in which their slaughter by the Han government resulted in severed body parts hanging in public display, ears, heads, penises. As part of their survival and maintaining their identity, they resent being referred to as *Chinese* or *minority*, especially by tour guides and in textbooks. They are *Miao*, but the government has been attempting to discourage that, mocking their linguistic resistance as nothing more than symbolic, ironic for a culture steeped in symbols.

On his ride across downtown Beijing this morning, painters were completing their work on a giant billboard celebrating the nation's minorities, right across the street from a sixty foot blown-up balloon of Ronnie McDonald in Lotus position next to its franchise on Dong Changan Jie on the eastern entrance to Tiananmen Square. There were some two dozen profiles of men and women with distinctive Han facial features and posturing like Hans, but they were all wearing indigenous costumes, a patronizing and condescending Han gesture in which these natives had been cloned and marketed as material accessories.

Ge remembered he had saved a few discontinued green two yuan bills with the two indigenous women on the front, and a backside that showed the Great Wall of China. He imagined the women were looking for a hole in the wall to escape from China and its Han domination as soon as possible.

13.

Next Sunday, Deng Xiaoping's black Audi with the 0000 black-on-white license plates picked him up at noon, earlier than usual for a one o'clock game.

—He wants to talk with you about some meetings next week, the driver explained.

Deng was working at his desk, and he confirmed it.

—There have been some complaints that my redefining the function of the Secretariat has sidelined the importance of the two major policy organizations within the government. They say because of that the Politburo meets less than once a month now, and that I have rarely convened a meeting of its Standing Committee.

Then he looked up at Ge and added, A waste of time and talent, just like the Americans, a terribly inefficient way to run a government, their separation of powers to what they say, check and balance each other all the time. And you know Chen Yun is deaf. What would two deaf people have to say to each other at a meeting?

But mostly he wanted to assign Ge to accompany his personal assistant Wang Ruilin who would be representing Deng and attending two meetings of the Secretariat the following week, an inner cabinet tasked with defining and vetting policy before circulating and re-circulating it between the Politburo and its Standing Committee for endorsement. To take detailed notes for the record, Deng clarified, to see what these high officials are thinking. But no matter, we need to go ahead and get the chairs together for the game.

Ge had started noticing that those in their fifties who had been exiled to physical labor and political rehabilitation in rural China during the Cultural Revolution, had been using that expression *no matter* as an idiomatic link with greater frequency this year, to get on with their normal lives as if they were in anticipation of another cycle of turmoil.

It turned out that there would only be a one-table game this Sunday instead of the usual two, as the others had meetings out of town. And since they were playing for low stakes, out came the scoring table, and the little square slips of paper for the players to write down their bids in the auction that preceded the play of each hand, an accommodation to Deng's difficulty of hearing.

The scoring table had been designed for players who wanted to make small wagers when they played the game. As a socialist approach to gambling, it was intended to even the competition and focus on the skills of the player rather than rely on the luck of the shuffle. It basically added up the sum of a player's face cards and aces to their partner's, and compared their raw score against what the chart determined they should have.

	Vulnerable	Not Vulnerable
20	0	0
21	50	50
22	100	100
23	150	150
24	300	200
25	450	300
26	600	400
27	650	450
28	700	500
29	750	550
30	800	600
31	900	650

	Vulnerable	Not Vulnerable
32	1000	700
33	1250	850
34	1400	1000
35	1500	1100
36	1750	1300

To score, add the total high card points from both hands, and check it starting with its match in the left hand column, then moving to the next appropriate right column against your raw score. Multiply the difference by two and divide it by ten to produce the final score. If the difference is greater than 600, the score is 12+1 for each 100 over 600.

Example one, vulnerable:
   Total high card points from both hands = 27
   Contract is 2NT making 4, for a raw score of 180
   Table score reads 650
   Difference is 650 – 180 = 470
   470 x 2 and divided by 100 = 9.4
   Opponents get 9.4 MIMPS

Example two, not vulnerable:
   Total high card points from both hands + 19
   Contract is 6C making 6, for a raw score of 920
   Table reads 0
   Difference is 920
   920 x 2 and divided by 100 = 18.4
   You get 18.4 MIMPS

At the friendly game in Deng's home, they usually played a low-stakes one yuan per 10 IMPs, and normally no player lost more than five yuan for six hours of playing, since the losses and wins were divided between the partners. A rather inexpensive form of entertainment while keeping mentally alert. Add to this a dinner between the two sessions, usually pork, shrimp or chicken *jiǎozi* and one-hundred-year-old preserved eggs, something Ge had avoided his entire life because of their coppery taste.

But something felt very different that night. Both Deng and Ge said very little during the normally social hour between the two sessions of *qiáopái*, and everyone avoided drinking their favorite *Maotai*. To Ge, Deng did not play his usual strong game, his concentration seemed distracted. These Sunday games were his escape from the complicated politics at Zhongnanhai, but perhaps not today. He twice wrote down an insufficient bid on the bidding paper, and pulled the wrong card from his hand once. Their combined game was mechanical and uninspired, resulting in each losing nearly twenty yuan.

It's the second meeting in Zhongnanhai of the Secretariat that Hu Yaobang had convened that week. Nicknamed *Cricket,* Hu was often the shortest person in the room, even when Deng was present. Ever the hard working and dedicated party member, he had collected, collated and by special CSB motorcycle couriers circulated to the entire committee the documents that the individual members had separately drafted in the last two days. At the end of the contentious discussion of the last meeting, he had tasked them to submit their written suggestions on the major national issues that should be discussed and ways to reach a consensus between the liberal and conservative factions before they were presented at the next annual plenum meeting of the party's Central Committee coming up in a few weeks.

—After all, Hu said at the end of the meeting at one in the morning, we must vet the issues and forward our consensus to the Standing Committee.

Ge was relieved that the meeting had come to an end. It wasn't easy for him to take notes of a brawl, trying to find out both what each committee member was literally saying verbatim, word for word, and trying to find the real or imagined meaning of their words, for the record, as Deng had repeated to him last week just before the *qiáopái* game at his home.

Earlier in the meeting Ge recalled Hu's previous appointments as Chairman of the party and then its General Secretary, someone who had supported liberal economic reforms that agitated many conservatives who were not hesitant to label him a *bourgeoisie liberal,* especially when he proposed reducing the military's inflated budget. The nagging question came up again for Ge: *how do I present the truth, in this note taking process that attempts to record what everyone is saying.*

He wondered if his attempt to record small truths in a world of big lies would be changed by a simple turn of the kaleidoscope years from now when researching historians focused their lens on his archived notes. *What am I to do with symbols, sarcasm, irony, conceits, metaphors, parables, aphorisms?* During a short break in the meeting, he recalled reading about the young immutable Qing Emperor Tongzhi of a century ago being shadowed in the less-than-a-block-away Forbidden City by notetakers describing his every move and recording every word he uttered.

He thought that novelists might also be notetakers of those truths between facts, further complicating his work, especially as he believed that good novels have to be something people would actually believe and perhaps would even change their lives; he was reminded of the American Ralph Ellison's *Invisible Man* which he had finished reading just last night. There was something important about the book that was beginning to change the way he looked at Beijing and what he was doing in it and who he was. Like Alan Paton's *Cry, the Beloved Country,* which he first read years ago while studying literature in Beida, where he first learned that we are what we read. There were more bookstores now like Wangfujing Xinhua and Foreign Languages Bookstore just across the street in downtown carrying more books in English like these on their shelves, even those by Kafka and Borges.

At the meeting today, it appeared to Ge that the Secretariat's members were attempting to decide what was important for the party and the government to work on, and what was not. But he couldn't be sure.

—After all, Hu reminded them, in Ge's words, *they'll be presented to the two hundred-and-some member Central Committee. [Editor's fact check: with the one hundred alternate members, it's actually a total of at least three hundred. This was probably Hu's oversight as it's unlikely that Ge, who lived by numbers, would make this numerical error.]*

53

At this meeting Yao Yilin appeared to Ge as the hardliner at the front of the conservative position. Though born in Hong Kong, Yao joined the party and participated in its December 9, 1935 student demonstration when 6,000 students from Tsinghua and Peking Universities marched on Tiananmen Square and demanded the Kuomintang government cease secret negotiations with the Japanese. They presented a list of six demands, including freedom of speech, press, and assembly and cease its attack on the communists. The Military Commission at Zhongnanhai responded with sabers, whips, sticks and water cannons.

—Comrade Hu, Yao said at one point, standing up and looking straight at him though he was addressing the entire committee, their personal assistants, and in some cases their own notetakers. I think it'll be very helpful to be reminded of the Four Cardinal Principles, so we'll stay the course and not veer from our responsibility. They are one, Keep to the socialist road, two, Uphold the dictatorship of the proletariat, three, Uphold the leadership of the Communist Party, and four, Uphold Marxism-Leninism and Mao Zedong Thought, he recited, before sitting down very slowly and deliberately, looking around the table making sure that everyone had paid attention.

Ge did not know how to handle this one besides writing down Yao's speech word for word. He looked at Yao with feigned interest and felt he was back in elementary school and the teacher had just scolded the entire class for its silent rebellion in their note taking.

For historical accuracy, Ge then decided he would first record verbatim what each speaker said, especially words from the conservatives or their office directors, but at the same time he'd try to memorize their physical gestures, what their eyes were looking at when they were speaking and when they were not, the changes in their voice, tone and tempo of speech, all of which he would later add as marginal notes next to the words in his written record of this meeting. At this, he felt he was perhaps writing a novel.

Following very specific instructions from the Central Security Bureau's director, Ge's at the Holiday Inn Lido on a side street a short kilometer or two from Capital International Airport. He's here for another meeting, this time with Deng's PA Wang and a Mr. Tze wearing an earbud, a security specialist out of uniform from CSB's Unit 8341. They were there to meet with the hotel's management to examine its security for an upcoming Chinese Contract Bridge Association tournament in two weeks that Deng and his team would be playing in, and to host to special guest, the Australian Denis Howard, the president of the World Bridge Foundation headquartered in Switzerland, who wanted to look at Beijing as a possible site for a future Venice Cup or Bermuda Bowl.

They had planned on taking the elevator to the hotel's main office on the third floor but when the elevator doors opened they were greeted by Beijing's top hit song that was being played in all the elevators of all foreign hotels and shopping centers:

Moon river, wider than a mile.
I'm crossing you in style some day

They decided to take the stairs and, perhaps prompted by Andy Williams' Splenda-infused version of *Moon River*, Wang asked, They did mean two in the afternoon on the second day of the second month, didn't they, you know, two, two, two?

—And if you wait a few minutes, it'll be two twenty-two and you can add two more twos, Ge joined in, not missing the opportunity to play with the numbers.

With outstretched arms, Wang stopped at the landing and added, If we wait four more years, today will be Tuesday, the second day of the week, and we will then have *er, er, er, er, er er,* he ended by imitating a Peking opera singer mocking Pŭtōnghuà in falsetto.

Up to this point it seemed to Ge that Mr. Tze from Unit 8341 had been so quiet and calm while taking a visual inventory of everything around them and then assessing its potential security threat, that Ge wondered if he didn't play *qiáopái* when he wasn't working. But Mr. Tze couldn't take Wang and Ge's banter any longer and had to join in.

—You sound like two morons. No wonder your security needs to be guarded and protected. And to think you actually run this country. The country needs to be guarded and protected from you, he said and lifted a wrist to speak into a microphone.

Just at that point, a woman's voice came up below them, accompanied by the clacking of high heels on the concrete steps.

—Ge, wait, Ge. I saw your name on today's guest list.

Ge recognized the voice and *gwáilóu* accent immediately. It was Ginny, her Pŭtōnghuà that she learned from language tapes in California made by missionaries to Guangzhou whose vocabulary and idiom had not been used in China for a century, at least not in Beijing. Ge had not seen her at the flea market for several weeks now, and her partner William—working alone looking for potential converts and still handing out those free green vinyl-covered New Testaments—had mentioned that she had been looking for another job. Wearing a tailored, dark brown sheath dress suit now, hair shortened into finger weaves, eye makeup, light blush, and lips painted lustrous red. No more floral printed cotton dresses and running shoes.

—I am Virginia, she reached out and introduced herself to Mr. Tze and Wang. I will be your guide around the building this afternoon. And you, Ge, you didn't tell me you speak English, she said and tapped her manicured nails on the notes on her clipboard.

—You didn't ask, Ge replied in English. What about you, he asked, disbelieving the transformed Ginny name and all, standing in front of her.

—I left ESEC, never believed it.

She explained that she's now the Holiday Inn-Beijing's liaison with corporate headquarters, and that she handled all its correspondence in English and consulted on ad copy for the media.

Two hours later, both Mr. Tse and Ge decided that they were uncomfortable about establishing adequate security at the Lido. Too many doors and outside windows, they explained to Virginia, who was busy taking down their comments. Especially troublesome was the group of raucous Germans at the main downstairs bar who had just been served their beer by a bartender delivering it on a long wooden rack holding six gravity-defying steins. They looked suspiciously at the four of them walking by, three Chinese men with a *weiße Frau*, before one of them made an undisguised racial slur and all of them picked up their steins spontaneously and started singing in unison at the top of their voices,

Ein, zwei, drei, vier,
Lift your stein and drink your beer.
Drink! Drink! Drink!

—Don't pay any attention to them, Virginia said. They're here every day at four prompt. They live in those apartments just behind this hotel.

When the group left the Lido they were unanimous in their assessment that the tournament had to be moved, probably to the Great Hall of the People on the west side of Tiananmen Square.

16.

On the last Saturday of February, the World Bridge Federation president's flight from Narita landed two months ahead of the annual Gobi Desert dust storm that whips and darkens Beijing sometimes for weeks, sometimes forcing school closures and cancelling flights. As Deng Xiaoping's partner for the entire three-day tournament, Ge had been invited to Howard's welcoming luncheon at the Great Hall of the People before the start of the *The Oldies* match, the nickname given in acknowledgement of the high number of nationally seeded players in this main open pairs event. It was also known that on Sunday Howard would be conferring the WBF's gold medal award to Deng, in recognition of his contribution to the development of *qiáopái* in China.

But on Sunday a man was creating a disturbance with a bullhorn on the northern steps before the main doors to the Great Hall. Ge had arrived early, and he recognized him at once, a *qiáopái* player by the name of Nie, who had been caught cheating in the last tournament and found guilty by the Chinese Contract Bridge Association. The penalty included a one-year ban from its tournaments and sanctioned club games, and his membership would only be reinstated if he were to rehabilitate himself and admit his treachery in a public act of self-criticism.

A large crowd was beginning to gather, and the traffic on Xi Changan Jie was starting to slow down, the beginning of a gridlock in the middle of the nation's capital.

Mr. Tze with the earbud from Unit 8341 was also there, and he nodded to Ge and said to him, this does not look good.

A few moments later, Mr. Tze walked away and spoke into the microphone on his wrist, shaking his head.

As Nie's self-criticism got louder and more contrite, and as the crowd grew larger, Ge knew that the tournament was going to have to be cancelled, or at least moved again.

—Yes, Mr. Tze confirmed. We can't guarantee the security here. Luncheon and tournament all moved to Beijing Hotel. Not far, walking distance, just across the street, really.

Ge was astonished, again. Things can and do change that fast in Beijing, even a major event such as this one that had been scheduled for the Great Hall of the People months in advance. Then he was reminded that it was an event involving China's preeminent leader, after all.

But he was going to be late for that lunch; he wasn't going to miss Nie's self- criticism for cheating at *qiáopá*i. He had heard the rumor that Nie had been caught leaning to the left and right at the table and peeking at his opponents' cards, but Ge was curious how he was going to confess his sins in the heart of the nation's capital. How would he sustain the crowd's attention and interest, especially when he wasn't using any big-character poster, the traditional dissident, protest, and self-criticizing theater of Tiananmen Square?

Waving his free hand and shouting into his bullhorn Nie repeated, I was bad, I was very bad. I cheated, I cheated, many times.

Ge thought that was not going to be enough. Nie had to say more than that to satisfy the CCBA's expectations for re-habilitation. Tiananmen Square was a good, traditional site for political self-criticism, but perhaps not for confessing to cheating in *qiáopái*.

But that was only the beginning. Nie then continued and said, I cheated at cards, cheated.

He peeked, peeked, he continued. To win, he had peeked at his opponents' cards. To win. And he played many card games. Cheated in all of them, all. *Dou dizhu*, *madiao*, open-face poker, even mahjong, when the players were too drunk to notice.

Next he explained the card game of *qiáopái* to the crowd that didn't seem to understand a word of what he said, playing with a partner, both cheating. Both. First we showed each other how many hearts we had with the same number of fingers on the front of cards we were holding. Like this, Nie demonstrated, holding three fingers on the front of the bullhorn grip, three hearts.

Next he said he tapped his partner's shoe under the table, with a numbered code, which he said they forgot sometimes, and then going down the list with assorted cheating strategies he and his partner had used in the last two years: holding the cards in front of the chest to show a maximum value for a bid, in front of the belt a minimum, and in between a middle; signaling what to lead by the placement of the scoring pencil pointed in a certain compass direction on the table, or the position of a cigarette lit or unlit on the ashtray to show partner what to lead, pointed at the partner for a club lead, to his left a diamond, to himself a heart, and to his right a spade.

Ge was beginning to be disturbed by this list when he recognized that beyond the peeking method Nie first mentioned, the rest were all well-publicized cheating scandals that had rocked international competition in the last decade by British, Italian, Israeli, American and German national players. It appeared Nie's self- criticism had now turned into group confession. Ge then imagined a Hong Kong Jungian analyst trained in Zurich could charge a hefty fee for designing strategies for self-criticism for clients obsessed with looking for their identity and their motherland and mother tongue, true or imagined, on either side of the Taiwan Straits.

Nie continued: the use of coughing when it was his turn to bid, the coded number of short coughs reflecting which suit he had a void in and asking his partner to lead it, and no cough showing no such shortness; removing the cards in their hands and replacing them in the same hand or in the other hand in a certain position to show one of the six major distributions of the thirteen cards dealt into four suits; and as dummy peeking into an opponent's cards and signaling the number of trumps held by the number of times he tapped his wrist; and the placement of the bidding cards in a coded pattern.

Finally at the end of this long litany of cheating strategies, Nie came to the end of his self-criticism.

—I was bad, he said, very bad. And I will not cheat again, not ever.

To which the crowd that by then numbered in the hundreds applauded loud and long, even though they had not understood a single word of what Nie had said, nor did Ge, who knew that most of it had never happened to Nie in this baffling self-criticism.

17.

On his way to his letter-writing job at Panjiayuan one morning, Ge's bicycle chain broke right in the middle of the Qinghua and Xueqing crosswalk in the busiest intersection in Haidian District, with a swarm of idling bicyclists waiting when the traffic lights were red in one direction and another swarm jostling through in the other direction along with a chaos of retired professors out walking their grandchildren, several obedient dogs all named *Kafka,* a few horse-drawn fruit carts and hundreds of impatient and inattentive students rushing to class at any one of the dozen universities nearby. Ge knew he didn't have time to go back to the apartment to find the extra pins, links, and tools needed to make the repair himself, so he wheeled his bicycle over to the repair and knife-sharpening hut set up on the southeast corner of the intersection.

Several students were ahead of him with flat tires, broken chains, and the one in the front of the line arguing with the repair specialist.

—I can't pick your lock, aiiieeeee, the man with the grease-covered work apron said to the student. I repair bicycles, no tool to break lock. How can you lose your key? Students today not so smart. You want me to just knock it open with a hammer, no?

Against that clanging noise, Ge got to talking with the student in front of him who was concerned about what kind of job he's going to get when he graduated in June.

—My party political guide won't talk to me and won't tell me what little reports about me he keeps in his secret file about me, even when he lives just two rooms down from me in the same dormitory, he said as he kicked at the flat tire on front of his bicycle.

—Things have not changed much since I was a student, back there, Ge said, pointing down Qinghua Road behind him, which could be Beijing Forestry University, Beida, Tsinghua University, Beijing Language Institute No. 2, China University of Geosciences, or China University of Mining and Technology, each of them with an identical concrete statue of the helmsman Mao Zedong with the breeze flipping up the lower flap of his military trench coat, either with his right hand waving, or both behind his back; each one measuring exactly 7.1 meters tall and counting the base, 12.26 meters, the numbers mandated in 1967 by the Tsinghua University's Red Guards to correspond with the founding date of the Chinese Communist Party on July 1 (7.1), and Mao's birthday on December 26 (12.26).

—He might just assign me to some job not in my field of study, in a failing state enterprise in some remote southwestern province, unless I find some way to give him some money. The corruption begins here.

Then he asked Ge about what he did for a living.

—I studied math at the university, number theory, prime numbers. Now I am a card player, and the probability table is my banker, Ge lied to him, but he did it to suggest that there were other options to make a living besides being a fixed wage-earner working in a state-owned enterprise, when the new economic policies that open up the market would eventually wrack havoc on the tenure of this rice bowl. Really then, what is the probability for a more suitable job for this student from the distant southwest mountainous province of Yunnan from which he is trying desperately to escape?

But in fact Ge's mind was somewhere else entirely. Recently he had been questioning the usefulness of the six major distributions [*Editor's fact check: he is correct, 4.4.3.2 for 21.55 %, 3.3.2.5 for 15.52 %, 1.3.4.5 for 12.93 %, 2.2.4.5 for 10.58 %, 3.3.3.4 for 10.54 %, and 2.2.3.6 for 5.64 %.*] of thirteen cards into four suits accounting for a probability of 78.7 percent of the time, in the process eliminating the practicality of the remaining ten-plus distributions of probability of 21 percent most of the time. He had been playing with the possibility that just the distribution pattern involving two suits holding 4.4 and 3.3 and 2.2 totaling a 71-plus percent probability—with the remaining cards falling into place soon enough—might be just as important, easier to work with, and more relevant to defensive card play.

He sensed that this graduating student was more concerned about government surveillance and control over his economic future than the political. Add to that the rising crime rate for robbery, burglary and even urban banditry, the huge influx of rural immigrants competing for jobs, and the rising inflation rate in the last two years: all contributed to the young people's terrifying outlook on their economic future.

Ge wanted to say something helpful to him but he could not find the words. When the student's flat tire had been repaired, the two of them said their goodbyes and well-wishes; the student looked at Ge as if he could not believe that Ge was a gambler, and in turn Ge wondered about the probability that this student would find a meaningful and fulfilling job and succeed in his desperate attempt to escape from his birth place.

In the late afternoon on his way home from work Ge decided to stop and talk with the bicycle repairman. He had noticed earlier that he had not charged the student much for fixing his flat.

—You charged him only one mao, Ge asked.

—Yes he said he knew that this student did not have very much money. He's not from Beijing or Shanghai; his accent gave him away, he explained.

—When his rich classmates go to class, if they attend class at all, they're chauffeured in a fancy American or German sedan. You won't see them on a bicycle.

—Motorcycles maybe, he continued, when they go to a drinking party on a weekend. And he's not one of those Crown Prince children of high-level party officials. They go to Beida, Tsinghua or Beijing Foreign Studies and get the top jobs in the country, Shanghai, here or the emerging Shenzhen.

Just before Ge got back on his bicycle in time to the changing traffic lights, the man had removed his work apron and had started closing and locking up the boards on his repair stall.

—I can feel it, he said, the winds from the Gobi will come early this year. There will be much dust and darkness from the unusually severe winds, and the schools will close like never before.

18.

Ge was there, and he was the notetaker when Mike Wallace flew to Beijing with his television crew for a long, sit-down interview with Deng for CBS's Sunday television news-magazine *60 Minutes*.

The far-reaching negotiated subjects with advance text for the interpreters began with Wallace addressing Deng as *Mr. Chairman*, an error that made Ge, interpreter Zhang Weiwei and Deng's PA Wang all blink in total surprise, but which was completely overlooked by Deng. No matter, he must have thought, having lived through the turmoil of the sixties' Cultural Revolution and in the seventies' attempt twice to revital-ize the proletariat revolution; we must forget it and just get on with our lives.

Wallace's first question asked what Deng thought of General Secretary Mikhail Gorbachev's recent speech given just seven hundred miles away in Vladivostok, a city that was ceded to the Russians in the First Convention of Peking in 1860 in one of its three Unequal Treaties that ended the Opium Wars.

Deng's answer was non-committal, but he said he was open to a continuing conversation and willing to meet with Gorbachev. After all, this was an informational interview, not an interrogation. And he basically presented the same answer to the next question regarding the normalization of relations with Vietnam. Deng was completely prepared for the ques-tions about the reunification of Taiwan, taking a strong posi-tion against both President Carter's and Reagan's interference in this domestic issue, he made sure about that.

Most of the interview focused on economic developments with Wallace beginning with, *To get rich is glorious*. That declaration by Chinese leaders to their people surprised many in the capitalist world. What does that have to do with communism or Marxism?

Deng's long answer started with a historical survey of the uneven distribution of wealth before the establishment of the People's Republic of China in 1949, going through several painful periods of adjustment with the intent of eliminating poverty for everyone, until he said, to get rich in a socialist society means prosperity for the entire people.

—To be frank, he added, we shall not permit the emergence of a new bourgeoisie.

Next, Wallace focused on the current inflation problems.

—You have been criticized several times that your policies for opening up the economy are going too fast, that the plans for eliminating state-owned enterprises will create both an intolerable inflation for most people as well as increased unemployment to make the situation worse.

Deng was ready for that one, having received the exact same criticism at home several times in the last twenty years.

—We are developing plans to avoid that, but in the meantime we expect some people and some regions will become prosperous first, like the cities and provinces in the Special Economic Zones. Much of it depends on outside help and their willingness to invest in China. Apple in Shenzhen, for example. And just look at the Pudong neighborhood east of the Huanzpu River in Shanghai, just waiting to be transformed into China's twenty-first-century flagship of economic development. That is my trump card for China's modernization.

After waiting for Wallace's interpreter to finish, Deng continued. Construction on the world's largest dam will soon begin on the Long River, and we are negotiating with several foreign companies who are interested in investing in this project, before ticking off a number of Canadian, American, Swedish, British and French corporations and ministries: U.S. Bureau of Reclamation, Siemens, General Electric, Électricité, U.S. Army Corps of Engineers, the American Consulting Engineers Council, Bechtel Civil and Mineral, Coopers and Lybrand, Merrill Lynch Capital Markets, Morgan Bank, World Bank Asian Development Bank, and individual foreign financiers. Japan has been very helpful, sometimes for free, he added at the end of the long list.

Somewhat perplexed by the details in this answer that was not anticipated from looking at the advance text, interpreter Zhang was starting to nervously tap his right forefinger on his knee; in his notebook Ge, tried to describe the astonished expression on the normally unequivocal and professional Mike Wallace.

Toward the end of the interview Wallace said, I understand that you are quite a bridge player, and that both President Yang Shangkun and Secretary General Hu Yaobang also play the game. Do you partner with them?

—No, Deng said quickly. No, he repeated, we play different games, but over the years I've partnered with Comrade Hu on the same team a couple of times.

19.

Over the years Hu had been a very reliable player, but not tough enough to be ranked an Oldie by the CCBA. He had tried out new bidding systems, much as he had supported liberalizing economic and political policies. He was theoretically attracted to C.C. Wei's Precision Club, and later the Italian Blue Team's Super Precision based on it, or the less-complicated Neapolitan Club; but he could not find enough partners who were open enough in their thinking or patient enough to try out and master these new bidding systems with him, especially those players who were also conservative party members still resistant to developing new political or economic policies to promote government transparency and to hold officials accountable for their mistakes.

Over the years Ge had played against Hu and his partner in pairs game a few times, but Ge thought they were always struggling with the Precision system that worked to their disadvantage, getting them into the wrong contracts and wary of each other's bids. But today he's at Zhongnanhai's archives to familiarize himself with Hu's position on Tibet and education reform, as he'd be taking notes at a meeting of the Politburo Standing Committee that Hu will be attending. Since Hu was pressured to resign as General Secretary two years ago because he was seen as being too lenient on intellectuals at universities who were asking for political reform and curbing the profiteering corruption of government officials at all levels, he had been distancing himself from Zhongnanhai, lost weight, and attended meetings of the Standing Committee of which he's still a member only when its main agenda featured an issue that he thought was important enough for him to be present.

Ge located the relevant files concerning Hu's official visit as the Party's General Secretary to the Tibet Autonomous Region in May of 1980. The official reports attached to the minutes of the Standing Committee meetings that he called when he returned to Beijing from Lhasa showed that he was so deeply disturbed by what he saw that he sent hundreds of Han cadres packing immediately and required the remaining ones to learn the Tibetan language. At these meetings he initiated provisions to increase funding to support Tibet's infrastructure, particularly its education and health programs, with the goal of empowering the Tibetans to control their own culture and to govern themselves. The last entry in the files confirmed that he had made a public apology in Lhasa for what China had done in its occupation of Tibet.

This took Ge's breath away. This was not going to be an easy meeting to take accurate and complete notes of, and it was likely to go on all night. Most people think that history is orderly and develops in a linear and coherent narrative, but as notetaker Ge was beginning to believe it is more likely that this narrative is often devastated by random natural events such as volcano eruptions, earthquakes, catastrophic impact extinction from an asteroid, as well as those deliberate and violent human acts such as occupation and war.

The meeting that started with a serious discussion on the main agenda item, Tibet and the territorial integrity of China, soon turned into a land grab for every hectare left on the drawing board, with those completely for it and those completely against it. Soon it turned into a brawl that went on all night. Ge could hardly keep up with his notes and interpretive comments on these notes on in the margins. The voices were loud, angry, fingers wagging and pointing, everyone except Hu and Zhao standing up and talking at the same time.

—You're a traitor, someone accused Hu, though Ge could not see who had said it, but thought it sounded like Yao Yilin's voice. You play *qiáopái*, he yelled louder, and use C.C. Wei's Precision bidding system. He's not even a good player, only a strategist and a traitor, born in Zhejiang but ran off to New York, then invented Precision and trained and led the Taiwan team to use it to come in second twice in the Bermuda Bowl. Traitor. Traitor. Traitor.

Then Premier Li Peng insisted on decorum for the meeting. Sit down, he said, everyone sit down. We can only hear one person talk at a time. Take your turn, he insisted.

Everyone sat down but Yao, who continued, and you abolished the position of Chairman of the Chinese Communist Party. That destroyed one of our nation's Cardinal Principles, To uphold the leadership of the Communist Party. That is treason.

Li, the Soviet trained hydrologist, ever the conservative engineer who thrived on stability, continued to call for order and attempting to reach a consensus before recommending it to the twenty-four-member Politburo as a national policy. But Ge noticed that Hu and his successor as General Secretary, Zhao Ziyang, were the only two who had not said anything at all in the ten hours of this long and arduous meeting with no resolution in sight, nor had they touched the cups of tea steeping in front of them, as if they believed that this stability that Li was promoting was only an illusion.

It was the first Thursday in April, and outside the Zhongnanhai meeting, the winds from the north continued unabated, pelting Beijing with dust and darkness.

In the darkest hour at three in the morning, Li made the decision to end the meeting for a day of rest, and announced that it would continue on Saturday morning, ten sharp, for the entire committee of five, their office directors, personal assistants, and notetaker, this last to accommodate Ge.

20.

On Saturday at ten sharp, everyone was there: the five Politburo Standing Committee members Yao Yilin, Zhao Ziyang, Li Peng, Qiao Shi and Hu Qili, accompanied by their office directors, personal assistants, and Hu Yaobang for his testimony on Tibet and education reform. In light of the brawl at the last meeting two days ago, Yang Shangkun and Bo Yibo were also present as observers from the extra-constitutional Elders, who under the direction of Deng made all the major decisions for the country.

For this meeting Ge started a new notebook, carefully spacing his words, distinguishing what someone said verbatim and his summary of it, especially those marginal notes that were now beginning to include some analysis of what the people were saying and trying to say, the fragility of words on words.

On developing the paper on educational reform that woud be recommended to the Elders, Hu Yaobang was quite specific in recommending the elimination of those government cadres involved in the monitoring of university students not only for what they studied, but also what they read, what organizations they belonged to, how much they partied, and the secret dossiers they kept for each student that would determine not only the student's job assignment, but the job location as well. Ge noted in the margin Hu Yaobang's Hakka background and how he had never attended school but had taught himself how to read as a child, adding *shortest person in the room who knows the importance of education.*

He was joined by Hu Qili who proposed the establishment of uniform national standards for teacher certification, narrowing the gap between rural and urban education, especially by increasing the funding for universities to make them more accessible, and encouraging independent research.

Not surprisingly, these proposals were supported by Li Peng, who had to travel to Moscow to complete his education as a hydroelectric engineer, which he later relied on for his administration of the construction of the Three Gorges Dam. His vote assured the needed majority for the Standing Committee, the other two following in line right behind Li.

No loud voices, everyone sipping their tea quietly, no one scribbling notes, not even Ge, until Hu Yaobang appeared to weaken, got up and interrupting a review of the Ministry of Education's budget, requested permission to leave. But the small frame of his body slumped back into the chair, his face ashen, his right hand drawing a half circle in the air.

His personal assistant leaned over him, taking his pulse, and Zhao asked if anyone had nitroglycerin. The National Defense Minister Qin Jiwei, who had a heart condition, gave him two from his pocket and with help moved Hu to the floor. Moments later a call went out to Liberation Army Hospital 305, just a block away from Zhongnanhai.

21.

A week later Hu passed away and his body was prepared for a memorial service to be held at the Great Hall of the People. Within hours of the announcement of his death, Peking University students pasted posters on the walls of their campus mourning his death, and, keping alive the long tradition of gathering in Tiananmen Square to memorialize the death of a beloved leader in the heart of the capital, hundreds of students went to lay commemorative wreaths at the Monument of the People's Heroes the next day, mindful of not obstructing traffic on the busy Xi Changan Jie.

Two mornings later on April 18, the tenor of the students' grieving acquired a new sense of urgency when hundreds of students from both Peking University and People's University staged a sit-in in front of the Great Hall of the People at dawn. They presented seven demands they insisted must be received by a high ranking member of the National People's Congress. This list included the government's full support for Hu's position on liberal political reform, admission that the past rightist campaigns against spiritual pollution and the bourgeoisie were mistakes, publication of the incomes of party leaders and their families, the institution of free elections, the establishment of freedom of speech, increased funding for education and faculty salaries, and lifting the ban on demonstrations. They also insisted that the government must respond immediately to their demands and publish and broadcast their list.

Such was the reportage by the Xinhua News Agency which doubled as a news-gathering organization, including summaries of foreign press coverage about China, as well as its more important role in providing and distributing all the classified intelligence collected by both the State Security Ministry and the People's Liberation Army to all the significant state agencies' and ministries' directors every week, and daily to top Party's officials such Li Peng and Deng Xiaoping.

—Look at this report, Deng interrupted himself impatiently while he was assigning Ge to a number of committee meetings he had to attend to take notes this week. And look at this list from the students, he added, flapping the list of demands at Ge.

Ge looked them over, and saw the hand of the usual Xinhua reporting of events, full of details but no analysis or interpretation of meaning.

—These will keep these meetings noisy, Ge said in wonderment before he left Deng's study. I'll have to bring an extra notepad.

An hour later Ge was handed this same list of seven demands, but this time they were on a crumpled piece of paper a homeless migrant worker had pulled out of his pocket as he balanced himself on the small folding stool at Ge's letter writing stall at the flea market.

—Some eager students were passing these out at the square when I crossed it to get here. What does it say?

Ge listened carefully as he had to negotiate yet another thick southern accent. Then he read it quickly; it was identical to the list list he saw an hour ago in Deng's study. Sensing the worker might have problems with some of the abstract concepts in the list of demands, he took his time and patiently explained each one to the worker who nodded knowingly. When Ge was finished with the list, the worker sat back for a minute, silent. Just when Ge was about to explain the list again, the worker put his right hand down hard on the little table between them before picking up the list and asking, and how is this going to help my family?

His family was in debt, he explained, having had to borrow from a neighbor the last two years during the severe drought that had kept them from working in the millet fields, before asking Ge to write his letter for him.

> *Beloved Parents,*
>
> *Please don't worry about your son. You will know I am well when you examine this message. It is I who wish you both health and strength, and every member of the family peace and safety. Enclosed is five yuan.*
>
> *Do you remember neighbor Xi? I have much trouble with him. He makes up story you have borrowed much money from him in last two years but never returned a fen. He tells everyone here this story from time to time and with such vivid details that all his listeners believe him and blame me. He brings shame to family.*
>
> *If it is true you have borrowed from him, please give me a clear account so I can manage to start returning the money to him. I am earning a small wage and can finagle some from my pocket.*
>
> *Your respectful son*

After Your respectful son left, Ge read the list of seven student demands again, and in many ways agreed with the need for them. But he also thought that they were not carefully thought out, and reflected the inexperience of the first- or second-year students who grew up as their family's youngest child or the only child since the One Child Policy went into effect in 1980, especially for urban areas. Unlike previous generations of young people in this modern century who were well-organized when they marched their demonstrations and petitions to Tiananmen Square, from the spiritually-possessed Boxers at the beginning of the century, to the May 4, 1919 and December 9, 1935 protests, to the decade-long murderous terrorism of the Red Guards, the students this morning appeared to be undisciplined with no organizational skills, these freshmen and sophomores who had been sheltered and spoiled by their parents and grandparents as little princesses and emperors, members of the Me-Me-Me-Me Generation with the Nike Air Jordans and Sony Walkmans who were setting up their own student committees independent from the accredited student campus organizations, sometimes several different committees in the same dormitory, in some instances each floor having its own with a membership of three or four. Ge saw confusion and trouble ahead.

22.

Late in the afternoon, the students in front of the Great
Hall of the People with the list of seven demands were joined
by students from Tsinghua University, Beijing Normal, Beijing University of Science and Technology and the Central
Academy of Fine Arts. They carried banners and shouted
slogans and rhyming couplets against dictatorship and au-
tocracy, praising democracy and science, keeping the 1919
May 4th tradition alive, and the students from the Central
Academy of Drama released helium balloons that read *Yaobang will never die.*

By ten that night, the crowd had grown to ten thousand,
with more than half of them Beijing onlookers and migrant
workers attracted to the students' political theater. By late
afternoon when no one had yet appeared from the National People's Congress to receive the list of demands, the entire
crowd moved a few blocks down to the Xinhua Gate at the
west entrance to Zhongnanhai, where Li Peng was attending
an emergency meeting of the Politburo.

Having cut short his visit to Tokyo, he flew back to Beijing
just in time to participate in a wide discussion that focused
on assessing the domestic and international response to Hu's
death. The meeting's attention was interrupted by the second
night of loud shouting, scuffles, and the singing of the national anthem *March of the Volunteers, [Editor's fact check: written
in 1934 by poet and playwright Tian Han who was later imprisoned during the Cultural Revolution. It replaced L'Interna-
tionale as the People's Republic of China's national anthem in*

1949.] the words of which were loud and clearly discernible inside the meeting in Zhongnanhai.

Arise, ye who refuse to be slaves;
With our very flesh and blood
Let us build our new Great Wall
The peoples of China are in the most critical time
Arise! Arise! Arise!

Li Peng and Zhao Ziyang, like everyone else in the conference room whose attention was interrupted by the singing, continued to disagree on the appropriate response above the drum beat of the song.

Ge scribbled *nothing new here* in the margin of his notebook.

—Comrade Zhao, we must be resolute and firm with these trouble makers, Li directed his comments at Zhao again.

—No one has been hurt, there has been no looting, and no property has been destroyed. Better we remain calm and not escalate the confrontation.

—But they will only see our forbearance as weakness, Li reaffirmed. Our security agents have noticed the presence of domestic and foreign *black hands* at work here, agitating the students and encouraging them to break the law, he claimed. We cannot just sit back and do nothing.

Ge circled *black hands* and ran a line from it to the margin, where he added *terrorist? spy? migrant worker? foreign journalis?, American literature teachers?*

Zhou ignored the repetition and used his seniority as General Secretary to lead the meeting to reach some consensus that would not demand too much compromise from the majority of the Politburo members, and to send them as recommendations to the Standing Committee.

So the group worked out their differences and agreed to instruct the Minister of Education to meet with the university presidents and ask them to normalize their campus activities, urging them to temper the students' inclination toward protest and demonstration, and to instruct the directors of the People's Armed Police, the Ministries of Public Security and State Security and Beijing's Municipal Police to encourage their personnel to remain calm and reasonable with the demonstrators as they enforcedddd the law.

Unanticipated by the people at this meeting, the very next day Deng would independently place on alert the People's Liberation Army's 38th Group Army based at Baoding just three hours southwest of Beijing, including its armored division, just before attending a memorial service honoring Hu at the Great Hall of the People, where Zhao would present the short memorial address.

On the very next day, to show the nation that there were no disagreements among the nation's highest officials, Li Peng saw Zhou off at the Beijing Railway Station as he was leaving for a state visit to North Korea. In order to maintain the appearance of national stability, Deng informed Ge for his notes that he had instructed Zhou not to cancel his trip to Pyongyang.

—We may have some splits at the top, but our government is strong and will not fall apart, he promised.

But Zhou was not so sure. As the train was about to leave, he said to Li, please feel free to call a meeting of the Politburo if you need to.

The harsh winds from the north seemed to have ceased for the season, but on the day after Zhou's departure, Peking University students formed an intercampus student organization, the Autonomous Federation of Students, and started a national boycott of classes, beginning with fifteen thousand on their own campus.

23.

Inside the Great Hall of the People almost all of the Party officials including Deng held a memorial honoring Cricket, at last released from its Chinese matchbox.

Outside, more than 200,00 students, workers and citizens listened to the broadcast of the short, twenty minute service on the square's public loudspeakers. What they didn't hear were the three directives Zhao made to Li Peng with Deng's endorsement on how to handle the demonstrations.

—First, now the memorial service is over, Ge recorded verbatim Zhao's instructions in his notebook, social life should be brought back to normal. We should firmly prevent the students from going into the streets and demonstrating, and we should get them to return to classes as soon as possible.

—Second, we must at all costs avoid any incident of bloodshed, because if such an incident should occur it would give some people the pretext they are looking for. But we should use legal procedures to punish severely all who engage in beating, smashing, and robbing.

—Third, we should actively adopt a policy of persuasion toward the students and hold multilevel, multichannel, multiformat dialogues with them.

Ge noted in the margin Li's agreement, and tried his best to record what he said verbatim, but he was not able to complete the entry as his attention was distracted by Li Zhao who was standing next to her husband's coffin and quietly blaming several of the officials around her that Hu had died because of how the Party had treated him in his sixty years of service to his country.

—It's all because of you people, she said, her eyes accusing each as she looked around her at those closest to the coffin.

Then it was moved slowly and out the back entrance, avoiding the students in the front who had petitioned the coffin be driven once around the square so that they could pay their last respects before it was transported to the Babaoshan Revolutionary Cemetery in western Beijing.

For several days after Hu's burial in Beijing, the newspapers, magazines and television programs throughout China continued producing Hu's obituaries, and Ge started to wonder if these perfumed linear obituaries that avoided Hu's encounters with contradictions, deceit, outright lies, betrayals and absurdities were the early keepers of China's history. Or more likely, the stories assembled by the Xinhua News Agency and distributed weekly to the directors of all the major state agencies and ministries would be washed, dried, spit-ironed, and returned to Xinhua a week later as press releases to be published as scooped news and outsourced to the entire world. Or if the official historian would come along and vet and edit them before they are recycled and inserted into the school's history textbooks. And what will happen to the letters, diaries, journals, memoirs, secret or otherwise, read or not? Will they be found years later by children or grandchildren and sold as scrap paper by weight? Or used to wrap fish at the open market? Once a piece of paper is used, by ink or lead, pen or brush—these attempts to understand the daily dose of incoherent and stressful and betraying and slothful and repetitious encounters in the media controlled by the State Administration of Press, Publications, Radio, Film and Television—it loses its value, and can be sold, as at some markets on the east side of Beijing, like the Panjiayuan flea market where Ge has his letter writing stall. Historians would do well to go to Panjayuan and purchase kilos of this paper and rummage through them for the real memory of China.

And what will happen to his notes and the letters he wrote for the migrant workers? Will they be included as part of Deng's papers and archived in Zhongnanhai with restricted access? Or will they become lost, just as people don't seem to remember what happened to them or their parents in this nation where amnesia is an essential survival strategy?

But not everyone. Not Li Zhou. Ge was to learn later that, unhappy with her husband's burial at the final resting place of China's revolutionary heroes in Beijing, Li Zhao successfully petitioned the government to allow Hu's ashes be flown to Gongqing and buried in a specially designed pyramidal mausoleum in a city he founded back in 1955 that was now energy self-sufficient and produced no harmful pollutants.

And not the three students who had been kneeling for three and a half hours since the memorial started at ten, waiting for an audience with Li Peng about the list of seven demands they had copied in ink and brush onto a long scroll that they kept in a bag in front of them. Li never appeared, and in the early afternoon two Great Hall of the People custodians came out and talked to them, after which they left the steps and rejoined the other students in the square.

24.

On the very next morning, Your respectful son was waiting for Ge at the flea market. He didn't want another letter written for him, he explained, but he wanted to talk to Ge about the list of student demands, flattening out the crumpled list on the small folding table with his palm.

—Again, I asked yesterday, what will this do for me and my family, he repeated, pointing to the list.

Then he said patiently to Ge, that his family has been farming for many generations, and for emphasis, he crossed the index finger of his right hand over its mate in the left before saying, ten exactly, with me.

—We are poor. I still can't read, but my children are learning a little in the small school a long walk from our home.

Then he looked around them and continued in a whisper when he was sure no one could hear him. Our leader Mao has made us all alike, every one poor. First they took away our small plots of land and said we all have to work together. Then they took away all household things made of iron, woks, washing basins, kettles, and sent half of us to work at the factory. Then p*lough deep, better soil,* they said, and next, *plant them close together, better harvest,* they said, and next *kill all the sparrows, they eat all the seeds,* they said.

—But none of that worked, he continued. All lies. But we were too afraid not to obey.

Then he said soon after the harvest got smaller and smaller; the factory made nothing useful for them. With no wok and basin left for the cooking and cleaning, his whole neighborhood had to eat and clean up together in a dormitory, like everyone else in the village. When the harvest grew worse by the year, and the seed-eating insects' population exploded, there was less and less for Your respectful son's family to eat. Many of his relatives died, including his sister, in the big famine that lasted for three years.

—It is a little better now, we can still be happy sometimes, but it is still hard; we still live from season to season. There was a long pause before he continued. When we are working in the fields, we still sing the same song we have for generations. It has changed very little in hundreds of years. I will sing it to you?

Looking into the dull red distant sunrise through Beijing's pollution, Your respectful son started singing.

[*Editor's note: these lyrics were translated by Z.Y. Kuo, and appear in his book* Chinese National Character and the Myth of Communism.]

Comrades have their new shoes on and kick about,
Cadres have their tummies filled.
For the farmer, his arms are skinny,
And face and legs all swollen up,
And every bone of his water buffalo sticks out.

At the end of this section, he was joined by two others down the line who had approached Ge's stall to form a trio of voices.

I toil day and night, year in and year out,
But my rice jar is empty and the fire of the cooking stove out;
No shoes to wear and my buttocks uncovered.
I still have to walk about;
Flesh has left my arms and legs,
And if I have one marrowy bone,
I certainly doubt.

I have looked and looked,
For a few grains of rice in the bowls.
I found nothing but water,
I am furious and bitter,
Beat me to death, if you wish, comrades,
But toil for you again? Never!
They say we have a bumper crop,
And other farm products are all up,
But for the whole year I have not had enough rice to fill a cup,
Today I harvest the paddy
Tomorrow my rice bowl is empty.

When they finished their singing, they shook their heads and went back to their place in line.

Ge was stunned by these lyrics, and from them understood the reach of this worker's question about the students' demands that he repeated this morning.

—You see, he explained, why are these students demonstrating? What do they want? They will have good jobs, and will have family and free school and free clinic for their children. They will never be hungry. Even the soldiers who protect them, their tummies will always be full.

Ge looked at him, but could not find a word to say, before the worker continued.

—All the revolutions this century now have been started by people like those students in Tiananmen Square, and they have fucked up every one of them, so that there will be another one in a year, or two, or ten, same thing.

—And we, we also stupid. We grow food they steal from us to fill their tummies to kill each other while we starve during autumn's full moon and try to make it to the next planting to repeat the entire cycle again.

—And you, you are like them, but a little different. I see in your eyes I can trust you. I trust you will write down my words to my family exactly, that much I can tell. Someone in my family one thousand lis away will find a way to read and understand what you write, my daughter maybe. But don't shed tears for us; we have done enough of it already, trust me.

After this man left, Ge quickly wrote the letters for the two workers waiting in line, then closed up his stall and rode his bicycle west, until he got to Nanhu Lake to the west of Beijing. He needed some time away from the density of downtown, and found a rock to sit on and look toward the hills further west, and thought back about who he was, what he was doing now, and if he wanted to continue doing what he was and living in Beijing.

He was born in his paternal grandparents' home in the small town of Shiyan near Xi'an, and after his young sister died at the age of four in the great famine, the family moved to Tianjin for a new start where G's mother taught mathematics and his father classics. They did not have much money, but enough from their teacher's salary and free housing in a small two-room apartment that was always filled with books, and plenty of paper to write on. But that life was interrupted by the madness of the Cultural Revolution, and the family managed to escape to Shiyan and hid out for a few years until it was safe to move back to Tianjin.

Compared to the singing worker, Ge thought he had lived a privileged life, even with the pain and loss of his sister. But now who was he? And what was he doing? Had the vowel that was added to his name changed him? Was he still the same person? Now part of him was Deng Xiaoping's *qiáopái* partner, and his personal and official notetaker as well, with a pass that allowed him into any meeting or archival vault in Zhongnanhai, the inner offices of the Great Hall of the People, as well as any collection deep in the basements of both the Museum of the Chinese Revolution and the National Museum of

Chinese History on opposite wings of the same building in Tiananmen Square.

Ge was beginning to have doubts about what he was doing, but he was not sure where he was going with this thinking. Sitting there on a rock and looking at the calm Nanhu Lake, Ge thought his country was becoming a place in which knowing the direction the wind was blowing across the lake could mean the difference between life and death. At this, he left the lake to go back to his apartment to pick up the materials he needed for taking notes for a Politburo emergency meeting in Zhongnanhai, called by Li Peng one day after seeing off Zhou Ziyang at the railway station. Reports about the student protest and demonstration were streaming into Zhongnanhai from both the State Security Ministry and the Public Security Bureau, and the Xinhua News Agency was sending its summaries of the foreign press coverage of the events in Beijing that were beginning to spread to other parts of the country.

But the meeting started with a report of a discussion between Beijing mayor Chen Xitong and the presidents of most of the universities in Beijing, in which they focused on plans to educate the students and dissuade them from boycotting classes and demonstrating in the streets. But Chen concluded that meeting was useless, given what happened today.

—Today nearly fifty thousand students in thirty-nine schools are not in class. The turmoil on campus has started to spread to the rest of society. The outlook is grim.

Ge did not feel his notes were completely accurate this evening, and there were no notes of analysis or clarification of meaning in the margins. As much as he tried to focus on what he was doing, part of him was still thinking about the meeting this morning with the singing farmer and whether he wanted to continue taking official notes for Deng and playing *qiáopái* with him. These distractions were beginning to result in some errors in his note taking, an incomplete phrase here, abbreviations, omitting the speakers' formal addresses to each other, *comrade* this, *comrade* that, but nothing that would alter the meaning of the meeting, which sounded more like a venting of the most conservative and vocal Politburo members' resolute opposition to what these students were doing.

Chen's dim view of the situation was joined by Li Ximing, who cited an intelligence report that Peking University physics professor Li Shuxian, wife of the astrophysicist Fang Lizhi [*Editor's note: Li and Fang sought political asylum at the U.S. Embassy in Beijing on June 5, until Henry Kissinger negotiated their release fifty-five weeks later.*] was a *black hands* agent acting behind the scene and fomenting trouble, encouraging and talking to the students and helping them get organized, particularly the freshmen, first time away from home.

Another Politburo member, Wan Li, referred to the Associated Press and Reuters reports that the students were continuing their boycott of classes, that they were not going to let their demands for freedom and democracy end in defeat, and the Japanese newspaper *Sanki shimbun* compared the student movement to the anti-government uprisings in Hungary and Czechoslovakia in the fifties and sixties, during which Chairman Mao persuaded the Soviets to drive their T-34 and T-54 tanks into the square of Budapest and put down the protest by force.

—Disgraceful, disgraceful reporting. They only interviewed selected students, only the loudest eighteen-year olds who know nothing, freshmen from Peking University forming their own illegal independent student organizations.

Li Peng continued this long list of diatribes against the students.

—There's a new student organization formed every hour. At Peking University there are at least four illegal ones, the United Students Association, the Association of Peking University Students, the Autonomous Federation of Students, the Solidarity Union and, he paused to nudge his thick black plastic eyeglass frames higher on his nose, and each has its own list of demands. This new one calls for the immediate resignation of all leaders older than seventy-five, an end to using the nation's tax monies to fund the activities of our Party, and establishing a cleaning committee to investigate corruption at all levels of our government. This is nothing but a naked declaration of war against the Party.

The final insult to the students came from Chen.

—These brilliant engineering students from the Beijing Aeronautics and Astronautics University are so far in space that they couldn't wreck their brains enough to conjure up a rhyming couplet that can be used at their rallies, he said, before reporting on the growing size of the student demonstrations.

—In size and intensity, he continued, this is unprecedented, and has spread to universities in twenty large cities throughout the country. Shake things up, create turmoil, boycott classes, fabricate rumors, attack the Party, attack socialism. Posters, handbills, they are even going into middle schools and polluting the minds of the next generation. At present, there are already sixty thousand students at thirty-nine universities here who are boycotting classes.

Ge hesitated at the number *sixty thousand*, and had to flip back two pages in his notebook to be confirmed that Chen had in fact said *fifty thousand* an hour ago, or at least according to his record, so he underlined *sixty thousand*, then circled it and drew a line to a question mark in the margin. [*Editor's note: similar to his note taking at the Secretariat meeting in chapter fourteen, it's very unlikely that Ge would make such a numerical error.*]

The hardliner Yao Yilin decided it was time to do something about these student bad elements.

—In view of the present dangerous situation of spiritual pollution and bourgeoisie liberalism, I propose we form a small group to halt the turmoil.

Supported by Standing Committee members Li Peng, Qiao Shi, and Hu Qili, the committee was capitalized to form a Small Group to Halt the Turmoil, and on a unanimous vote, Li was appointed to chair it. It was then charged with three responsibilities: to issue a full report about the protest and demonstration situation to Party Central and the State Council with recommended countermeasures to combat it, to instruct the Beijing Municipal government to mobilize the citizens to expose the plotters and resolutely organize a struggle against the enemies of the Party and socialism and, given the serious nature of the demonstration, to present a full report to Deng Xiaoping in the morning for immediate action.

To make sure the seriousness of these charges were understood and carried out, Yao included instructions to prohibit student intercity travel and the formation of student organizations, urging Party leaders in factories and mines to make sure that all the individuals in their work units clearly and fully understood the threat to the nation's stability presented by this turmoil, and to ensure that violators would be fully punished, with no exceptions. Proud of his amendments to the committee's responsibilities, and as a tribute to Deng Xiaoping that he would make the right decision tomorrow morning, Yao lit up an expensive Lesser Panda cigarette, Deng's favorite brand, made from the tips of the best tobacco leaves in his native Sichuan.

25.

Ge was waiting in front of his apartment building with his note taking materials in his book bag when the black Audi with the 0000 license plates stopped to take him to record Deng's meeting with the Standing Committee in his home. He arrived well before the scheduled nine o'clock meeting and went straight to Deng's study, where he interrupted Deng shuffling through and reading that morning's stacks of reports and newspapers with a cigarette in his mouth.

—We won't have time to go over your notes from last night's meeting, but I'm sure they will repeat every word of it in a moment. Just remember, I won't be able to hear what some of them are saying, and you will have to repeat it when I look at you, he said, pointing to his left ear.

When the meeting started, Deng sat in the middle of row six chairs opposite another row of six chairs with Li Peng sitting in its middle facing Deng. Ge sat with his notebook directly behind Deng's left side.

—We all feel that the situation is extremely grim, Li started the report. They are demanding that we reverse our verdicts on spiritual pollution and bourgeois liberalization. Then he said emphatically, Ge noted in the margin, the spear is now pointed directly at you and the others of the elder generation of proletarian revolutionaries.

—They are forming illegal student organizations. Reports show Peking University has at least three illegal student organizations, Association Solidarity Union imitating Poland's, Chen Xitong added.

—At Beijing Normal they are openly chanting *Down with Deng Xiaoping* and beginning to smash small bottles against you, some of them the very same bottles they had saved from displaying them to support your return ten years ago.

And then President Yang insisted that they could not allow a few people with ulterior motives to make use of this movement to manufacture turmoil, which Ge had to interrupt Yang to repeat in a whisper to Deng's left year.

—I agree completely agree with your decision, and we must explain to the whole Party and the entire nation that we are facing a most serious political struggle.

At that point Li suggested an immediate editorial in the *People's Daily* to get the word out on what Comrade Xiaoping had said, and the deputy chief of propaganda Zeng Jianhui got to work immediately drafting such a document, entitling it *The Necessity for a Clear Stand Against Turmoil*. It was edited by Li and Hu Qili on the spot, and the final copy approved by everyone in the room. Li then telephoned the Xinhua News Agency with specific instructions for its immediate release, before it was couriered by the CSB's Unit 8341 to the national radio and television stations to be broadcast that same night and published in the next day's newspapers.

26.

When the couriered document arrived ten minutes later at the Xinhua News Agency's main office at 57 Xuanwumen Street, the deputy director Fan Rongkang and six other writers made some minor formatting and layout changes and sent it downstairs to the printing department, which had set its machines on hold since Li Peng's phone call.

In the *People's Daily* then, in the next morning, April 26, first edition, the full editorial appeared in layout position one, on the top half of the front page, to be followed by its reprint the next day in almost all of the newspapers in the People's Republic of China. The staff also translated the statement from the Standing Committee to ten other languages for global distribution—English, Japanese, French, Spanish, Portuguese, Russian, Arabic, Tibetan, Korean, Mongolian, as well as ten internal minority languages.

> *The Necessity for a Clear Stand Against Turmoil*
> *...An extremely small number of people spread rumors, attacked party and state leaders by name, and instigated the masses to break into Xinhua Gate at Zhongnanha.*
> *...an extremely small number of people with ulterior purposes continued to take advantage of the young students' feelings of grief for Comrade Hu Yaobang to spread all kinds of rumors to poison and confuse people's minds.*

...Flaunting the banner of democracy, they undermined democracy and the legal system. Their purpose was to sow dissension among the people, plunge the whole country into chaos and sabotage the political situation of stability and unity. This is a planned conspiracy and a disturbance. Its essence is to, once and for all, negate the leadership of the CPC and the socialist system. This is a serious political struggle confronting the whole party and the people of all nationalities throughout the country.

If we are tolerant of or conniving with this disturbance and let it go unchecked, a seriously chaotic state will appear...

All comrades in the party and the people throughout the country must soberly recognize the fact that our country will have no peaceful days if this disturbance is not checked resolutely.

The article in position two on the lower half of the first page reported Tsinghua University's Peaceful Organization Committee's request for a meeting with high ranking government officials had to be aborted because no student showed up to meet with Liu Zhongde, deputy secretary general of the State Council, and Hu Dongchang, vice minister of the State Education Commission.

The next morning Deng invited his friends to his home for a game of *qiáopái* that night. Being a Thursday, it was to be single session instead of the usual double session of Sundays, a thirty-two hands match for two teams of two pairs each drawn randomly from four pairs. A friendly game, he promised everyone on the phone, with plenty of peanuts and dried plums and candy, and only one ¥ for ten IMPs, so that no one would lose much on a weeknight. And he asked Ge to be early, so he could give him his note taking assignments for the next few days before the important Mikhail Gorbachev four-day state visit in two weeks.

Ge had first heard the editorial on radio two nights ago, which was rebroadcast repeatedly the next day on several radio and read on Beijing's three television stations. He had heard rumors in his neighborhood's open market that the students were organizing to march around Beijing in defiance of that editorial the next day, so he avoided taking the Second Ring Road to Deng's home on Mei Langgu Street as that had been planned for the march. With the additional security checks along the way, he was late.

—Unexpected traffic in the streets, Ge explained as he removed his bicycle gear and brought out his notebook from his bag, more than I expected.

—No matter. Two meetings tomorrow: go to mayor Chen and Li Ximing's meeting with university presidents in the morning, and to Li Peng's PB meeting in the afternoon. Here are the details, and he handed Ge the schedule as well as two bulging surveillance files submitted by the Ministry of State Security and the Xinhua News Agency and stamped *RE-CEIVED* two hours ago.

Since the other players had not arrived, Ge sat down and opened the file. On the top were some notes that Xinhua reporters had put together when they attended several march-organizing meetings and interviewed several student activists on the campus of Peking University, Tsinghua University and Beijing Normal University. The students said that they hoped the editorial would rekindle student interest in their cause, as it seemed that it was beginning to wane after ten days of speeches and demonstrations with no result, not even a meeting with any important government official. Perhaps this editorial would reignite their interest and galvanize them into a coherent and effective course of action, one of them was quoted as saying, although the person was not identified.

They then decided that the best thing to do at that point was to organize a march around Beijing the next day, but to be very careful to conduct a peaceful and orderly march to create a positive impression not only to Beijing but to the entire world as foreign journalists and television crews were beginning to arrive, preparing background shots and cultivating selected diplomats and other journalists to be interviewed for the upcoming Gorbachev visit. And to take the Second Ring Road around Beijing and avoid going through Tiananmen Square. A penciled addition at the bottom of the last page of this report indicated that at least fifty thousand students were expected to participate in this march, not counting maybe twice as many ordinary onlookers, one of whom was quoted as saying what the reporting Xinhua journalist thought was a common public reaction, that the editorial had taken the student demonstrations too seriously.

Another Xinhua journalist reported that Beijing's university presidents were unanimous in expressing their sympathies for the students, that the editorial exaggerated the dangers of the demonstrations, and most of all, that it was divisive and removed the basis for any dialogue and negotiations between the students and the government officials. The final pages in the Xinhua reports noted that on most surveyed campuses, an average of two-thirds of the faculty did not show up for the government mandated reading and study of the editorial. One professor interviewed thought the demonstrations only pointed to the Party's mistakes that had prompted the students' protest in the first place.

The State Security Ministry section of the file reported a very different response from both the provincial political organizations and the military's political departments. Every single leader of these units reported total compliance in meetings to read and study the editorial. They all agreed, thought the editorial was timely, and with resolute dedication they committed to stay in step with Beijing to combat this turmoil. A few had additional suggestions on how to implement these general directives. One mentioned the necessity for additional funds to educate the students in the correct political thought, and a curious footnote from the Twenty-Seventh Army's [*Editor's note: the Twenty-Seventh Army, based in Shijiazhuang, is one-hundred-and-fifty miles from Beijing.*] report included tasking the government with the need to stop corruption in the Party and society, stop inflation, and to get rid of the job assignment system.

To Ge, the *qiáopái* that evening seemed dull, and he was distracted by what he had read in the surveillance reports before the game. But from experience he could call up the automatic and play his normal strong game, and would remember most of the cards in every one of the thirty-two hands played that night, at least for a week. But Deng did not appear to be distracted by the reports or what other possible turmoil the students could be hatching that night. He completely immersed himself into this match, one Lesser Panda after another. Two of the players on the other team did not do so well, and it hurt their score. In the end, Deng's players won six ¥ each from each of the four players on the other team.

28.

On Friday morning Ge went to take notes at the scheduled meeting between mayor Chen Xitong, PB member Li Ximing and the presidents of most of Beijing's universities at the Great Hall of the People, now protected by five hundred soldiers from the 38th Group Army.

Li started the meeting by alerting the presidents that they would be receiving the sixth notice this afternoon from the State Education Commission asking them to continue to educate their students and staff about the dangers of the demonstrations and their threat to the stability of the Party and the security of the nation.

The president of the Chinese University of Political Science and Law mentioned it was going to be difficult to follow that sixth notice. He said Zhou Yongjn, the chair of the Autonomous Federation of Students, had personally promised him that he would stop these demonstrations, but changed his mind, broke the promise the next day and was last seen out in the streets organizing. This flip-flop also happened on the Peking, Tsinghua and People's campuses as well, where the students were beginning to enter middle schools and factories to proselytize and recruit participants to their cause. Some of these students had even entered the many hutong neighborhoods scattered to the north of Tiananmen Square, to persuade their residents to publicly smash the little bottles they had saved from about a decade ago in support of Deng's return from his exile in Nancheng.

—You can imagine, he said, this creates a very dangerous environment for little children out walking and playing with their grandparents in streets littered with shattered glass.

Toward the end of this listless meeting, the presidents arrived at a consensus to encourage the government to crack down on corruption, to distinguish genuine patriotic expressions of the majority from the irrational rant of a disgruntled few, and a request for members of the Central Committee of the State Education Commission to meet with the students to hear their complaints patiently. Li ended it by reminding them that the cadres inside the Party must keep their heads clear and not let the students confuse them.

Ge then walked the few blocks across Tiananmen Square, Dong Changan Jie to Zhongnanhai for the meeting Li Peng had called for the PB to meet on the same afternoon, to discuss how to destroy the enemy and eliminate the student demonstrations. Mayor Chen started the meeting by reporting on the morning's meeting with the university presidents.

—One of them reported that the students had used their bicycle locks to close the large lecture halls so that students would not be able to attend classes. And the building janitors had all claimed that they didn't have any cutters strong enough to break these locks.

—See, see, Li Peng interrupted. They are taking away from the peaceful and patriotic students their right to attend class. The whole country responded vigorously to the editorial published three days ago, he continued, nudging his black plastic glass frames higher up on his nose. This turmoil is carried out by a tiny minority of bourgeois liberal bad elements linked to foreign anti-Chinese forces. Two days ago the standing committee of the governing Kuomintang Party in Taiwan publicly declared their support for the students, as well as the lead editorial in Hong Kong's *South China Morning Post*.

Still a bit tired from his morning's meeting, Li Ximing added that a few days ago a reporter from L'Agence France-Presse interviewed the Beijing Normal student Wuerkaixi, an Autonomous Federation of Students leader.

—He is only twenty years old and is a Uyghur. And probably a Muslim with their special diet too. How can someone like this understand strategy? He gets the worst grades at Beijing Normal. Some *black hand* has to be behind him. He's way out of control. We've got to expose them.

The meeting ended when all the PB members unanimously decided on a motion to call for the scheduling of two meetings, the first the next afternoon for a round-table dialogue between the representatives of the two officially sanctioned student organizations and middle level administrators in governance and education, and the second one to take place afterward between the same student representatives and Mayor Chen and PB member Li Ximing.

It was well past midnight when Ge got back to his apartment, the end of a long day in which he didn't think he had recorded anything at all worthwhile in his notebooks, and he was looking forward to working at the flea market early the next morning: at least the letters he would be writing would be personal, thoughtful and important.

29.

At the flea market the next morning Ge stopped by the newsstand on the corner across from his letter-writing stall where he would occasionally pick up a Shanghai newspaper or newsmagazine. The vendor was talking about Shanghai mayor Jiang Zemin sacking Qin Benli, editor-in-chief of the Shanghai newspaper *World Economic Herald,* for publishing some four hundred uncensored copies of its recent issue 439; he had been instructed in advance to delete some reports and interviews with students that were critical of Deng Xiaoping and included reactionary slogans. [*Editor's note: an electrical engineer, Jiang was appointed General Secretary of the Central Committee of the Chinese Communist Party two months later, and concurrently the chair of the Central Military Commission, and later served as the 5th president of the People's Republic of China elected by the three-thousand member National People's Congress, for the maximum of two five-year terms.*]

—Four hundred copies printed before Shanghai's Municipal Public Security Bureau stopped the press and seized what was left of those illegal copies, he said. Some made it to Beijing. I have three left, a collector's treasure.

One of the onlookers warned him to be quiet about it, before he's arrested and imprisoned for profiteering from trafficking in stolen state secrets.

Later, when Ge was finished writing the letters for the few who showed up that morning, he rode his bicycle to the Great Hall of the People to take notes of the scheduled meeting between forty-five representatives—from Ge's notes—from the sanctioned and legal All-China Students Federation and Beijing Municipal Students Federation, and a State Council spokesman and a vice-minister from the State Education Commission.

Yuan Mu—identified in Ge's notes as being close to Li Peng and a former Cultural Revolution activist—denied that there was any corruption inside the Party, or any government censorship of the news media.

—I have come to realize that a problem exists; namely, there exists in our party, state, and society a fairly serious phenomenon of corruption, said a young man who identified himself as a student in foreign languages at Beijing University of Aeronautics and Astronautics. The Central Committee talks a lot about this problem, but no firm measures have been taken. Therefore, he concluded, the students have strongly demanded that in handling this problem the central authorities see to it that policies are firmly implemented so as to let the students and people see the results.

—Once again, Yuan replied, on behalf of the State Council, I sincerely invite people from all walks of life, including the vast number of young students, to report cases of corruption involving any officials. They will be investigated.

Both SEC vice-minister He Dongchang and Yuan both avoided answering most of the questions raised by the student representatives, and ended the meeting within the hour after He's closing remarks.

—Please let me say a few words, he said. Regarding our students of schools of higher learning in the capital as well as students of the entire country, I, myself, and staff members of the State Education Commission, adult comrades, teachers and presidents of various schools all have the same frame of mind, that is, they want to love students as they love their dearest children. Even if the students make mistakes, we will help them correct their mistakes.

Later in the same evening, the taped recording of this meeting was presented to the entire nation during the extended evening news program by the national network Central China Television. When Ge heard again those last words, he thought that Yuan and He's parents had not potty-trained them properly before they were allowed to go out into life on their own.

The meeting the next afternoon between twenty-nine different student representatives from some seventeen universities and Beijing mayor Chen Xitong and PB member Li Ximing resulted in further obfuscation and denials of accusations that Party and government officials had embezzled state funds and accepted bribes to benefit their children. Fake news, they claimed. And again CCTV broadcast the entire meeting on its national network.

In response to these meetings shown on national television, there was more student unrest throughout China, amidst allegations that the students at these official meetings had been selected for their passive attitudes and modest views. This led to the establishment of more autonomous student organizations, more petitions and demands for selecting their own student representation for any future dialogue with government or Party officials, all the way until May 4, the anniversary of the 1919 student movement protesting the Japanese and German occupation of parts of China, and the government's weak response to the unequal treaties at the beginning of this century.

Under the banner of the Autonomous Federation of Students, a coalition of organizations produced a May 4 proclamation as the seventieth-year continuation of the movement started in 1919. It promoted the values of democracy, science, freedom, human rights, and the rule of law. Together with tens of thousands of other students from all the universities in Beijing, they left their Haidian District for downtown Beijing. Four hours later they walked into Tiananmen Square on Xi Changan Jie.

30.

The next day Deng's PA Wang Ruilin telephoned Ge to remind him that the Sunday *qiáopái* game was on this week, a double session sixty-four hand match with a short break for dinner.

—It'll start at one, he said, and added, everyone should be in good spirits. The usual one ¥ for every ten IMP.

And they were. The looming threat of economic and political chaos by the student demonstrations and disruption of traffic and business in Beijing and elsewhere in the nation seemed to have been tempered by the May 4 Declaration the day before that included a call to end the boycott of classes, as well as urging everyone to continue to negotiate in good faith for the resumption of dialogue between the students and the government. So they walked into Deng's living room in a jovial mood, and joked about China's chances in the World Cup next year.

—Fat chance, someone said. The last time we didn't even qualify when we needed only a draw with Hong Kong, with a population less than the city of Beijing. And they beat us two to one, right here in Beijing. Remember the riots after that? And claims that the match was fixed?

—But remember, someone pointed out, that Hong Kong has all those football-playing expats to draw from, Australians, Scots, Dutch, Portuguese, as well as that King George V High School's long inter-port winning record.

—But all we have to do is beat Qatar to qualify. They have a population the size of one of our large villages.

This raucous banter ended when someone pointed out, Yes, but, look at our football program. With so many players to draw from the world's largest population, our team has the worst record of not qualifying, and when we do, the worst losing record in FIFA's history of international play.

—There must be a reason, he said quietly, and looked around at everyone in the room but Deng.

—What did he say?

—He said Qatar has bought a good team this year, Ge leaned over and whispered into his left year.

Everyone played a good game in the afternoon session of thirty-two hands, and in the absence of any hand with a quirky distributional probability, the difference between the two teams at the dinner break was only twelve IMPs, a score that could be reversed by just one hand.

When the group sat down for the dinner, and perhaps tired of the earlier football discussion or concerned that its continuation would create some tension with Deng, the group took up an abstract banter about whether there were significant strategic differences between a pairs game and a team game. [*Editor's note: in a pairs game, one pair plays against every other pair in the competition; in a team game, one half of the team of four plays the exact same hand at one table against the other half of the other team at the other table.*]

Deng entered the discussion when he said, I don't think so, if the skill levels of the two teams are similar. They will be taking same chances, at least my partner and I do, and if their playing and techniques are at the same level.

—I agree, Ge said. I think the most important aspect of our game at our level of play is not to let anything distract our concentration on any hand, easy or not, competitive or not, especially in defense. This is quite a simple game, after all.

—You see, Deng interrupted, that's why I call him *Mr. Technician.*

The evening half of the match was almost identical to the afternoon, until the bizarre score that resulted from this hand.

```
              ♠ A3
              ♥ 9532
              ♦ J743
              ♣ QT5
              N
♠ 5                        ♠ KJT8
♥ AK64      W      E       ♥ QJT7
♦ AKQ85                    ♦ 9
♣ A83              S       ♣ KJ42
              ♠ Q97642
              ♥ 8
              ♦ T62
              ♣ 976
```

Deng and Ge sat North-South at their table, defending a 7♥ after a miscommunicated auction by their opponents, when East misunderstood West's splinter bid of 3♠ as a suit, and thereafter bidding 6♠ and corrected to 7♥ by West and taking all thirteen tricks with a 9♣ opening lead by South for a score of 2210 points. Sitting North, Ge did not dare double 7♥ for an opening lead of a ♠ by Deng, as he was not sure they played that coded convention.

At the other table their partner sitting East did not open the bidding, and consequently stopped at the contract of 4♥. With the same opening lead of 9♣, somehow he managed to take only nine tricks to go down one. Neither of them was willing to explain to Deng and Ge why they had misjudged each other's bids and stopped at 4♥, and how they managed to go down for a minus score of 100.

The net score of minus 2310 IMPs on that hand alone cost Deng and Ge the match, as well as 15 ¥ each.

On his ride back to his apartment close to midnight, Ge thought there was a flaw in his advice about not letting one's concentration in the game of *qiáopái* be distracted, when the partners were not understanding what each other was saying in the first place.

31.

The very next morning Ge attended a meeting of the Standing Committee at Zhongnanhai, chaired by General Secretary Zhao Ziyang just a week after his return from North Korea.

Ge's notes recorded Beijing Mayor Chen starting the meeting with a full update on the student activities since the May 4 Declaration last Thursday.

—Their declaration to the end of the class boycott was, in one word, deplorable. On the very next day, only half of the students at Peking University went to class, and the Uyghur troublemaker Wuerkaixi succeeded in keeping almost all the students at Beijing Normal from going to class.

As part of his report, he mentioned that the Peking University students allegedly voted Saturday morning to continue boycotting classes, and made a point of naming the troublemaker Wang Dan for speaking as the chair of the Autonomous Federation of Students to support the boycott. And Chen ended by acknowledging that the Peking University students just this morning had demanded a series of five conditions before they would return to class.

—One, he started numbering them. We must withdraw the April editorial and admit it was a mistake. Two, we must recognize the legitimacy of the Autonomous Federal of Students. Three, we must take measures against corruption. Four, we must restore Qin Benli to his chief editorship position at the *World Economic Herald*. And five, we must reconsider Beijing's ten regulations restricting demonstrations and marches.

Soon the meeting turned into another brawl between the conservatism of Chen, Li Peng, Li Ximing, and the more open Zhao, Hu Qili and the Elder Bo Yibo.

Led by Li Peng, the disapproving disciplinarian who continued to emphasize that this turmoil threatened the stability of the Party, socialism and the nation, the conservatives focused on the need to end these student demonstrations, separate the leaders from the patriots and punish them. The other more tolerant and patient group openly acknowledged that the unequal distribution of wealth as well as the high inflation that had lowered the standard of living for the vast majority of the nation reflected errors in the government's recent economic policies that had made the public lose their trust in the Party and the socialist system, especially when they saw high level Party officials and their children benefiting from them.

Ge recorded in the margin of his notebook an analysis of this meeting, that it ended with Zhao taking the ambiguous position supporting the need to distinguish the vast majority of students who were, he said, fervently patriotic from the handful of those who are intent on exploiting the situation to fish in troubled waters and create conflict. Then Ge circled "fish in troubled waters" and ran a line to the margin of the same page with an accompanying note that identified that this was a Zhao aphorism, word for word.

—I propose we place the contents of our meeting on the agenda for a meeting of the full Politburo for further discussion as soon as possible.

32.

Early in the morning toward the end of the week, Ge was picked up by the black Audi with the 0000 plates for a meeting at Deng's home to take notes of a consultation between the three most powerful politicians in China in early May of 1989, Zhao Ziyang, Secretary General of the Chinese Communist Party, Yang Shangkun, President of the People's Republic of China, and Deng Xiaoping, who, at the age of eighty-four, made all the final major decisions in a vertically structured government after extra-constitutional consultation with the group of eight Elders of which he was a member. Officially Deng only held the title of Vice-Premier and Chair of the Central Military Commission.

Even though it was a Saturday, when Ge arrived at Mei Langgu Street before nine, Deng was already absorbed by the stacks of reports and newspapers on his desk, with the surveillance files from Xinhua and the Ministry of State Security on top.

—Look at this one, he said, lighting up another cigarette and handing Ge the MSS file. See what it says about a hunger strike?

The file reported that in the previous two days, a group of Peking University graduate students had proposed a hunger strike in Tiananmen Square to greet Gorbachev, and another group was collecting signatures to invite him to visit the university as a guest speaker.

—They are smart, this hunger strike acted out in front of all the foreign journalists and television cameras here for the

Gorbachev visit. It will surely reignite the waning student interest and take attention away from the importance of our summit visit.

It was widely known that Deng had worked hard for this meeting for years. The Soviets had even agreed to Deng's pre-conditions for such a meeting, that they would pull all their troops out of Afghanistan and out of the zone north of their border with China. He had hoped that this meeting would thaw the icy relationship between the two most powerful Communist countries in the world for the last thirty years and normalize relations between them.

After the customary salutations for Zhao and Yang's arrival, Deng opened their discussion by saying that he believed the student movement was initiated by a tiny minority stirring up the great majority, with which Zhao immediately agreed, adding that they needed to separate the broad masses from those who were using it to fish in troubled waters, repeating the same aphorism he had used earlier in the week. Then he pressed for the necessity for holding dialogue with the students.

—Dialogue is fine, Deng interrupted him, but the point is to solve the problem. We're fumbling over what to do. The senior cadres are getting worried.

Then he named six of these Elders, Chen Yun, Peng Zhen, Li Xiannian, Wang Zhen, Sister Deng and himself. [*Editor's note: Sister Deng is Deng Yingchao, wife of Zhou Enlai and foster mother of Li Peng.*]

Next they discussed the general public's response to these demonstrations, and it ended when President Yang described the People's Liberation Army's position.

—The army is fully in line. These protests are not going to spread to officers or soldiers in the military.

Unknown to them at the time of this meeting, and at the same time of this meeting, the Autonomous Federation of Students announced at Peking University the start of a hunger strike to begin at two in the afternoon that same day. One hundred-and-sixty students wearing white headbands had taken an oath that was included in the afternoon report to Deng. An undercover MSS agent was posing as a journalist outside Building 29, where he recorded that oath.

> *I solemnly swear that, in order to promote de-*
> *mocracy in the motherland and to bring prosperity*
> *to the country, I will go on a hunger strike. I resolve*
> *to obey the rules of the hunger strike group and will*
> *not break my fast until we have achieved our goals.*

That same agent also included with his report a handbill prepared by the Autonomous Federation of Students entitled "Declaration of a Hunger Strike."

> *In this bright, sunny month of May,* it began,
> *we have begun a hunger strike. During the glorious*
> *days of our youth, we have no choice but to abandon*
> *the beauty of life. Yet how reluctant, how unwilling*
> *we are!*

This initial declaration was followed by a five hundred character explanation for the need of the hunger strike, closing with,

> *May the pledge that we write with our lives*
> *clear the skies in our republic.*

This was accompanied by a much shorter handbill by the title of "Manifesto for a Hunger Strike," which asked for public support for the students' agenda to achieve a more open and democratic form of government for the entire country.

The MSS report ended by describing that, by four in the afternoon, several parallel student organizations in separate groups had appeared at the square from the direction of Xi Changan Jie, two from the Peking University Hunger Strike Group that included the students with white headbands who had earlier that morning signed the oath, an independent group that ended up forming a circle north of the Monument of the People's Heroes, another group of students wearing white headbands on bicycles, and another group of students demanding a meeting with Gorbachev (scheduled to arrive in Beijing in two days), the AFS, the Dialogue Delegation, and several representatives of the strikers, student monitors, and student first-aid teams.

33.

The crowds of onlookers and students surrounding the hunger-strikers were getting larger and creating confusion at Tiananmen Square that made it difficult to distinguish the strikers from the non-strikers, and who was representing whom.

—We don't seem to represent anybody any more, a student from the Dialogue Delegation Committee answered in English to a question from a British Broadcasting Corporation journalist. As soon as we make the least bit of headway, they overrule us and nothing we said before counts.

With the international media paying full attention to the strike, the government organizations took a soft approach. None of the strikers were arrested, and students who had fainted were immediately taken by waiting ambulances to nearby hospitals. Later numbers from the MSS showed that during the ten-day period of the strike, more than eight thousand students were shuttled to these hospitals.

The government tried for two days to talk the students into leaving Tiananmen Square with the promise of further dialogue, to no avail. Consequently the welcoming ceremony for the arrival of Gorbachev had to be moved to the heavily guarded Capital International Airport.

—There were more foreign journalists and their cameras at the square than at the airport, PA Wang Ruilin informed Ge the next afternoon as they rode in the black Audi to the Diaoyutai State Guesthouse just south of the Haidian District for a meeting between General Secretary Mikhail Gorbachev of the Communist Party of the Soviet Union and General

Secretary Zhao Ziyang of the Communist Party of China. He was pissed.

Ge didn't ask for a clarification but circled "pissed" in his notebook and in the margin wrote *Gorbachev?* and *Deng?*

In front of the CCTV cameras, Gorbachev reported that he had a good conversation with Comrade Deng Xiaoping that morning, and that they were both satisfied.

—I appreciate the achievements of the Chinese people under the leadership of the CPC, he continued. Reform at the present time is no easy job. One cannot expect reform to succeed overnight.

Ge looked up from his notes on this last statement from Gorbachev, and decided to put two question marks in the margin next to it. Then he crossed them out when Zhao pursued this discussion.

—China's political reform should keep abreast with the development of the economic structural reform. It should be neither faster nor slower than the economic reform.

But it did not go any further, and it ended just before the banquet when Zhao said, What counts is to proceed from the basic tenets of Marxism in continuously developing theory and updating concepts along with changes in the situation.

Gorbachev would not let it rest, however, as he was quoted on the evening CCTV news the next day saying that he had been following China's reforms sympathetically.

—Economic reform would not work unless supported by a radical transformation of the political system. Without this a normal process of change is inconceivable.

34.

On his next free day from a note-taking meeting, Ge went to his letter writing stall at Panjiayuan. As he was writing a letter for a young woman, a group of three tourists stopped at the table next to him to chat with William passing out free green-vinyl covered New Testaments.

—Hey buddy, the man in shorts, knee high white socks and sandals with a big plastic shopping bag said to William. You look like you're American.

—Yeah, Omaha, here for a couple of years.

—We're from Tulsa, one of the women said. You look like you're doing God's work. They need it, all that trouble that's going on. So noisy around our hotel, non-stop day and night.

—You want to see the great deal we just got on the other street? The man lifted his red-white-and-blue vinyl shopping bag and pointed down the street.

Carefully he brought out a package, placed it next to small stacks of New Testaments, and slowly unwrapped a dark sculpture of a reclining woman and placed it on William's table.

—What is it?

—You don't know? the other woman asked. We've been shopping for a week here for antique Oriental treasures, and finally found it just now. This is a porcelain pillow.

—Great buy, the man with the sandals and white socks said. Only two-hundred ¥. A steal.

—What is it made of?

—See this, hippopotamus ivory, she said and illustrated it with a solid knock with her knuckles.

—It has a name too, *Doctor's Lady*, and comes from the famous Ming Dynasty with a certificate of authenticity. See? She brought out a piece of paper and unfolded it. At the top of the page was the title in English capitals, *CERTIFICATE OF AUTHENTICITY*, and it started with *Doctors Lady*, followed by descriptions of sensuality and romance and Hippopotamus Ivory. There were multiple ownership stamps across the bottom of the sheet.

Fake, Ge muttered to himself before continuing with his letter writing. There's nothing fake in these letters.

—Did he say something? the man asked and nodded in Ge's direction. But maybe not, he's just busy doing his thing with the girl.

—You see here, the man continued. Isn't this just wonderful, such beauty and tranquility, compared to the chaos of this new China.

—Yeah, this is what we came to see, this wonderful and glorious China.

Ge muttered to himself in English again, yeah, antiquity, in the middle of writing the next sentence.

The man was startled and asked William, Did he just say something in English? I'm sure he did again, nodding with his shoulder this time.

—I don't think so. I don't think he knows English. But you know what, I thought he was reading a book in English the other day, but I couldn't be sure as I didn't see the front of the book.

—And what's he doing with that girl?

—I'm not sure, and I've been here next to him since the beginning of the year. I think he's maybe writing letters for them.

—What? She can't write herself? What's wrong with her? In Tulsa everyone can write.

Again, Ge thought these simple constructed narratives so thick with lies were much easier to believe and perpetuate, like these tourists looking for the real China by searching for its antiquities in a flea market, or keeping Agfa and Fuji in business by photographing the hutongs or on the Great Wall at Badaling just an hour 's drive from downtown Beijing. Starting with the original lie of the wall itself, how it was constructed to maintain the political stability of the nation by keeping out the invaders and bad elements from the north, a lie resolutely sustained by one dynasty after another while the wall stretched longer and longer for more than a century until the end of the Qing Dynasty when it at last ran out of both real estate and lies for further development.

35.

On the Wednesday morning before Gorbachev's departure the next day, Ge was at Deng's home on Mei Langgu Street taking notes of a meeting of the Politburo's Standing Committee called by Deng.

Ge started his record of the meeting describing that General Secretary Zhao talked first, about the difficulty the fasting students were facing to make concessions.

—We have to get them to delink their fast from their political demands and get back to their campuses as soon as possible. Otherwise, anything could happen, and in the blink of an eye.

But Li Peng had something else in mind that he wanted to settle at this meeting.

—I think, he said, standing up and looking straight at Zhao across the room, Comrade Ziyang must bear the main responsibility for the escalation of the student movement, as well as the fact that the situation has gotten so hard to control. Furthermore, he has said that the students do not oppose our underlying system but demand that we eliminate the flaws in our work, thereby underplaying the turmoil and their threat to end our Party and end the socialist system.

—The movement has gotten steadily worse, Deng concurred. Before adding, After thinking long and hard about this, I've concluded that we should bring in the People's Liberation Army and declare martial law in Beijing—more precisely, in Beijing's ten districts. I am proposing this today to the Standing Committee of the Politburo and hope you will consider it.

—But Comrade Xiaoping, Zhao objected, it will be hard for me to carry out this plan. I have difficulties with it.

Ge pressed the words *big brawl* in the margin of his notebook, and circled it.

The meeting ended with three specific instructions. The SC would meet later that day to make the final decisions about implementing martial law. Li Peng was instructed to have a dialogue with the students the next day and ask the hunger strikers to leave Tiananmen Square. And the SC would report to Deng on the events of the next morning and to Party Elders on the progress of martial law deployments.

At the continuation of the SC meeting later that day, the brawl continued with Zhao asking if martial law were the only option, and Li Peng insisting that Deng had already made the decision on martial law a few hours ago and, since no one was going to change his vote on the implementation of martial law, and since the SC was deadlocked at two for it and two against, it was decided that the SC would return the next morning and present its decision to the Elders and Deng, effectively terminating the functioning of the SC on this matter.

36.

All eight Elders came to the meeting early the next morning at Deng's home, with Li Peng opening the meeting saying
that the SC was split on the decision to declare martial law.

—We old comrades are meeting with you today because
we feel we have no choice, Deng pressed on.

He then described the chaos that had dominated Beijing
and indeed the entire nation for more than a month, drawing
everything to a standstill while the students demonstrated and
marched. Nothing has been done, he said.

One by one everyone in the room believed it was important to be unified and unanimous in total support of martial
law, resolutely repeated and repeated all down the line with
no exception.

—These people are really asking for it, Elder Wang Zhen
said toward the end of this meeting. They should be nabbed as
soon as they pop out again. Give 'em no mercy! The students
are nuts if they think this handful of people can overthrow our
Party and our government.

They concluded the meeting by designating that martial
law would begin at midnight on Sunday and that President
Yang would be in charge of the martial law details and would
liaise with the two senior PLA marshals Xu and Nie.

37.

With the impossibility of car or bicycle transportation getting through the streets thick with demonstrators and on-lookers between Mei Langgu Street and Tiananmen Square, Ge had to hurry to get to the Great Hall of the People for a scheduled meeting between Li Peng and student representatives. The only car he saw in this neighborhood was the black Cadillac with the black 0224-00001 diplomatic plates that he knew belonged to James Lilley, the new American ambassador who'd been in town for less than a month. In addition to the five hundred PLA soldiers from the 38th Group Army already inside the building, additional security was provided by un-dercover CSB Unit 8341 plainclothes agents.

After clearing three separate security checks, Ge got into the large conference room just in time to see an official with a sheet of names introduce each of the eleven students to Li Peng, who greeted each one with a brisk handshake before taking a seat on a sofa with an official accompanying him on both sides and facing the students who were beginning to sit in a long row of chairs facing them. Ge stood to the side and away from the CCTV camera crews, taking notes and trying not to be noticed nor to create a shadow, ready for a big brawl.

—Delighted to meet you, Li Peng started. This meeting came a little late. I apologize for this. Then he set the agenda for the meeting, Ge wrote in the margin of the notebook. The topic I would like to discuss is how to relieve the fasting com-rades of their predicament as soon as possible. We look at you as if you were our own children, our own flesh and blood.

Stunned by this distracting alternative narrative, Ge was momentarily suspended with his thoughts about being in this Great Hall of the People for the second time in three weeks when a government official talked as if he needed further potty training, or at least provide some tips on fisticuffs for a decent brawl reminiscent of the Boxers of nearly a century ago.

But the Uyghur freshman Wuerkaixi from Beijing Normal was not at a loss for words. Dressed in a hurry with pajama bottoms, he was the first student to talk.

—The time is pressing, he said. You have just said that this meeting is a little late. The fact is that we asked for a meeting with you as early as April 22 at Tiananmen Square. Therefore, this meeting is not only a little late, but too late.

Several students, but mostly Wuerkaixi and Wang Dan, took turns addressing the officials sitting across from them and stressed the importance of an immediate, open, equal, direct dialogue, and more importantly, the retraction of the April 26 editorial, accompanied by an apology. They also set the conditions that would end the hunger strike: openly acknowledge that the student activities were patriotic and were extensions of the 1911 revolution, and that all future dialogue between them would be broadcast live on Central China Television.

38.

President Yang started working right away. He first called for and then chaired a meeting of the Central Military Commission that same afternoon, including the chairman of the People's Liberation Army's General Political Department, the PLA's Chief of Staff, and the director of the PLA's General Logistics Department. After developing the initial implementation plans, Yang went back to Mei Langgu immediately to report the details to Deng.

—How many PLA troops will be in Beijing? Deng asked, after Yang had completed describing the general assignment of responsibilities.

—18,000 at this point, counting the People's Armed Police.

Yang then handed Deng a copy of the specific troop deployments, which Deng glanced at and handed to Ge to copy for the record. Then without a moment's hesitation, Deng dictated to his PA Wang Ruilin the details of the martial order.

In accordance with Article 89, Item 16, of the Constitution of the People's Republic of China, [Editor's fact check: it reads (16) to decide on the imposition of martial law in parts of provinces, autonomous regions, and municipalities directly under the Central Government;] *the State Council has decided to implement martial law in parts of Bejing beginning May 21, 1989. The following units are ordered to deploy in designated areas in Beijing on May 19 and 20: the 24th, 27th, 28th, 38th,*

> *63rd and 65th Armies of the Beijing Garrison Command under the Beijing Military District, the 39th and 40th Armies of the Shenyang Military District, and the 54th and 67th Armies of the Jinan Military District, to restore order to Beijing and clear out Tiananmen Square.*

When Yang tasked the commanding officers of the three military districts to coordinate their specific routes in Beijing and times of arrival, he was informed that Xu Qinxian, the commander of the 38th Army that was headquartered only two hours southwest of Beijing, had refused to follow the martial order. He was immediately stripped of his command and taken to a nearby army hospital for treatment of his health.

—This is a military order. A soldier follows orders. Disobedience is not tolerated.

Yang next instructed the commanders that their soldiers were not to fire, even if provoked, and not to issue weapons at this point.

Later that same day, Beijing Mayor Chen Xitong signed additional implementation orders for Beijing. They announced that demonstrations, student strikes, work stoppages and all other activities that would impede public order were banned, citizens were forbidden from fabricating or spreading rumors, networking, making public speeches, distributing leaflets, or inciting social turmoil, and that any assault on the Party, government, or army, or radio or television stations was expressly forbidden.

39.

Deng called his usual Sunday double-session *qiáopái* game at his house three days after Gorbachev's departure from Beijing. Ge got an early phone call from the driver of the black Audi that he'd have to find his own way to Mei Langgu Street as all the roads were clogged with citizens protesting against the martial law and blocking key streets to keep the soldiers from the 38th, 63rd and 28th Army Groups from getting on Xi Changan Jie and approaching Tiananmen Square from the west.

—Even a bicycle would be impossible, he added.

So Ge had to leave his apartment early, leaving even his book bag and notebook behind. He started out taking the shortest line, but soon had to alter his route because of the blockage. At one of the intersections where some workers had erected barricades blocking trucks and armored personnel carriers, he saw several citizens talking with some soldiers in the back of a PLA personnel truck with wooden benches. They were trying to convince the soldiers to turn around, promising them that what was happening in Beijing was an act of patriotism and not terrorism.

—What you're doing is not good for our country, one of them yelled, and louder when he repeated it because the soldiers looked bewildered and sat silent in their mustard green uniforms.

They reminded Ge of the singing Your respectful son he had written a letter for, who came back the next day to ask quite reasonably how the students' demands for democracy were going to improve life for him and his rural family.

—Empires rely on violence to maintain control, the person who looked like an academic continued, before Ge interrupted him.

—Can't you see from the way they're acting, they're from the south? They don't understand your Pǔtōnghua. Get an interpreter, stupid one.

Disgusted with this intellectual, Ge turned away and tried to reach Mei Langgu in the most circuitous route in order to avoid any further encounter. Furthermore, he could not quite understand why Deng was insisting on keeping his weekly Sunday *qiáopái* game when he had been surrounded by escalating turmoil for almost a month now. And Ge worried about continuing to be Deng's reliable and trusted *qiáopái* partner in a game with its own structured conventions and rules was only a charade to mask the reality that Deng had completely lost touch with the very people whose interests he had stopped serving, at least in the last three years. Ge was also concerned about continuing to take notes as honestly and accurately as possible at these significant meetings. He believed that these notes as language could be misinterpreted and exploited by future Party historians with access to the secret archives in Zhongnanhai in order to construct a positive legacy for Deng.

—You seem to be distracted, Deng asked Ge after he had cleared the Unit 8341 security checks.

—I'm okay; those security agents were very thorough today.

—Yes, they wanted me to move into Zhongnanhai, but I said no way. Li Peng and Yang Shangkun have already moved there, for their personal security, but Li said it's only temporary.

Ge had never seen such terrible *qiáopái* in the first sixteen hands in the afternoon. In addition to an abundance of mechanical errors, pulling the wrong card, trumping partner's trick, the bidding was also awful, miscommunication that resulted in missed games and missed slams on both sides. When the two teams compared scores before the second sixteen hands of the first half, there were nine wild swings in scores on both sides.

On the last hand just before the half ended, Deng's PA Wang Ruilin went behind Deng and whispered into his left year.

—I'm afraid to tell you that we have to stop the game, Deng announced. We'll cancel these terrible scores and begin afresh next Sunday.

As soon as the six other *qiáopái* players had left, Deng said to Ge that a MSS messenger had just stopped by to report that a dozen Chinese University of Science and Technology students were headed in the direction of Marshal Nie Rongzhen's house.

—And look at this Ge, he continued, and opened a new MSS file that came with the messenger before handing it to Ge. The troops have been blocked at all points from entering the Square, the north, south, east and west. Some of them tried to reach the Square by the suburban subway, but students and ordinary citizens lay on the tracks by the throng.

Ge looked at the reports. In the hurry to implement the martial plan, the officers at the company level had not been given alternate route maps, and squads had not been assigned Pŭtōnghuà interpreters resulting in some scuffles from dialect misunderstandings at several major intersections on the west side of Beijing. Furthermore, the reports pointed out that most of these soldiers had insufficient crowd control training, and that most of them were young and came from the same rural backgrounds as those out-of-work migrant workers who had been streaming into Beijing at more than ten thousand a day over the last couple of months.

Another MSS file included a report from the Railway Ministry that showed sales of more than fifty-thousand discounted one-way student tickets to Beijing in the last week. The accompanying analysis showed that these out-of-town students did not want to be excluded from participating in Tiananmen Square in the national struggle for political reform.

Deng lite another cigarette and started shaking his head. He then asked Wang Ruilin to task President Yang to work with the Central Military Commission to pull back the troops to regroup, develop alternate plans to get to and control Tiananmen Square, and to call up the standby units to triple the PLA personnel to five hundred thousand.

When Wang returned from the communications room, he brought in an updated message from an Unit 8341 agent. Marshall Nie did not personally receive the CUS&T students' letter asking for his intervention, and responded by letter saying that the troops were in Beijing to maintain social order and encouraged the students to leave Tiananmen Square and return to their classes.

Discouraged, half of the students then went to Marshall Xu Xiangqian's residence an hour later and asked for his intervention on the belief that the soldiers were ordered to suppress those students who refuse to leave, and that their resistance would result in a bloody incident.

—We might do something now, and he asked to call for an immediate meeting of the eight Elders.

When they arrived an hour later, Deng announced that something had to be done to realign the positions at the center of the government.

—-The turmoil outside has occurred because the Party had dragged on and kept us from solving things that should've been solved long ago. So the trouble gets bigger and bigger, and now it's out of hand.

His corrective solution included two suggestions for their discussion and action. First, because Zhao Ziyang had gone soft and was too sympathetic with the students, he must be replaced as General Secretary. As well as Hu Qili on the Standing Committee: he's too close to Zhao.

—We need to think about who're the best comrades to replace them, and meet soon to discuss it and make a decision.

Next he sought the Elders' endorsement of three new directives for the effective implementation of martial law. And he immediately rattled them off.

—First, increase the number of troops. Second, call in the armored divisions. Third, arm the troops.

One by one, they agreed.

It was nearly three in the morning by the time Ge got back to his apartment. The streets were more crowded than earlier in the day, and more barricades had been erected, including dump trucks and overturned buses set up to prevent armored personnel carriers and trucks from getting through.

Ge was in a conundrum, and he did not like it. On the one hand he believed in some of the political issues the students had raised, but he also felt the conflict Your respectful son expressed. This was further complicated by seeing the bewildered faces on the soldiers in the back of the PLA truck this morning, and the scolding they took from the intellectual, berating them for their lot in the Chinese social fabric, this morning or a thousand years ago in the Northern Song Dynasty, Ge thought.

Walking in the dark, he also thought the country had somehow survived these last thousand years with one tempest followed by another. What is left, he asked, what is the real China?

But most of all, he was starting to think about how he had been living under a different name in the last thirteen years, and if that had changed him. And if so, what were his options?

40.

And indeed, Deng had called for another *qiáopái* game the very next Sunday, and Ge received the same call as a week ago from the driver of the black Audi.

—No vehicle traffic at all, you must walk. And no bicycle.

The walk took less time than last Sunday's, and no mustard-green PLA unit on foot or in truck was in sight. However, there were more street barricades, and the workers and students were beginning to use walkie-talkies to alert each other of troop movements. At Deng's residence, since he had refused to move into Zhongnanhai last week, the CSB had heightened its security with steel spikes and light machine-gun teams positioned at all the nearby intersections leading to Deng's home, which now had a row of concrete blocks surrounding it.

The two-session game appeared impossibly long to Ge. Every time he wrote his bid on the piece of paper being passed around, he would sneak a look at his watch to see what time it was. He found himself wishing PA Wang Ruilin would come in with another MSS or CBS alert that would require immediate action, starting with cancelling the *qiáopái*. He even looked across the table at Deng's packet of Lesser Panda cigarettes, but thought better than to ask for one. At one point he caught Deng looking at him for not saving Deng from getting endplayed, and decided to pay more attention to the game. It is a simple game after all, he reminded himself.

And Wang did come in with a MSS update just as the group was sitting down for their customary pork, shrimp and chicken *jiàozi* and one-hundred-year-old preserved eggs.

Deng nodded to Ge, and the two of them left the dinner table and went into Deng's study to look at the MSS file.

After leafing through the short report rapidly, Deng started laughing.

—Look at this, he said, the Central Academy of Fine Arts students are finally joining the fray. They're just over there, he pointed straight east, only a five-minute drive from here.

Ge looked at the file. The report indicated the students were almost finished with their project, a ten-meter-tall sculpture made with foam and paper mâché that they called *Goddess of Democracy*. The accompany MSS analysis reported that because of their need to complete the project in a hurry, the students had recycled an earlier frame, and had designed the new statue based on the revolutionary realism piece called *Worker and Kolkhoz Woman* that the Russian sculptor Vera Mukhina made for the 1937 World's Fair in Paris, according to an art historian.

—Why are we wasting our time over this? Deng asked. The State Security Bureau has already warned these students that any driver involved in moving this piece into Tiananmen Square will lose his license. So what if they manage to get it there?

So Wang shrugged his shoulders and apologized for interrupting the *qiáopái* game and left the group to play the second half of the match.

41.

Deng called a meeting of the Elders two nights later. The demonstrations appeared to have settled down a bit, at least in size, and the black Audi was able to pick up Ge for the meeting at Mei Langgu.

Just before the meeting started, Deng pointed to an open MSS file.

—Their statue is up. Somehow those students were able to cut it into six pieces and moved them by bicycle cart into Tiananmen Square. See this picture?

He held up a photograph the MSS had snapped of a photographer taking pictures of the students realigning the six parts of the statue and covering it with plaster.

—And they have aligned the statue in the axis between the Monument to the People's Heroes and Tiananmen gate, looking straight at the painting of Mao above its entrance.

Ge looked at the file, and noticed that MSS had identified the photographer, a Jeff Widener from the Associated Press, an American. It listed him as staying in Beijing Hotel's room 610 with an unobstructed view of Tiananmen Square and Xi Changan Jie's western approach into the square. The accompanying text also mentioned that most of the foreign journalists, photographers and camera crews had not left Beijing, even though the subject of their assignment, Gorbachev, had left a week ago. The file also included summaries on how these news agencies from America, Japan, Germany, France, Hong Kong and the United Kingdom covered this event.

—And look at this other file, Deng continued and handed a second MSS file to Ge.

This was a file that tracked Hong Kong's support of the student demonstrators, with a detailed timeline of their activities as well as an inventory of the supplies they had provided to the students and fake hunger strikers of the Tiananmen Square occupation. They included tents, medical supplies, bottled water, and a case of umbrellas, strangely enough, as it seldom rained in Beijing in the months of May and June. It also included donations for meals—especially for the out-of-town students—provided by the many Kentucky Fried Chicken and McDonald franchises around Beijing, especially MacDonald's largest one in the world on Dong Changan Jie's eastern entrance to the Square and only two blocks from the Beijing Hotel.

When the other seven Elders arrived, Deng initiated the discussion by outlining the agenda's focus on realigning the Party's leadership team.

—Let's begin by discussing a new leadership team for the Center. Let me give you my view and see if you think it's correct.

He mentioned that the commonly anticipated replacement for Zhao Ziyang would be Li Peng, but he thought that Li would not be the ideal candidate, as his negative and aggressive attitude toward the students would not make him an acceptable leader.

—Perhaps a better candidate would be Jiang Zemin, he suggested. Just look at how he handled the turmoil at the Shanghai newspaper *World Economic Herald* by shutting it down immediately. Shanghai has to be given a larger role at the Center.

—But not to worry, he added quickly while lighting up a Lesser Panda. I will talk to Li Peng personally. We can give him both the dam project and the space project. His golden parachute. That should keep the engineer in him happy.

One by one each one of the seven Elders took their turns supporting Deng's candidate: Chen Yun, Li Xiannian, Peng Zhen, Yang Shangkun, Bo Yibo, Wang Zhen, even sister Deng Yingchao resolutely endorsed Jiang Zemin. There was no dissension, or much of any discussion. Ge thought of a mathematical concept he had learned in his number theory studies at Beida years ago, something akin to zero-sum strategy, or cooperation probabilities, or the Abilene paradox of mutual consent when in reality no one agreed. They all amounted to the danger of rocking the boat, or self censorship, or the group-think that was accumulating in front of him. And he remembered the deterministic mathematical language for the tell-or-defect equation suggested by the game theory's handling of political decision making: really simple, as if there were only two players: $P = \{Pcc, Pcd, Pdc, Pdd\}$

On the ride back to his apartment Ge wondered if the Elders' words would freeze once the truth was about to come out, their silence reflecting the desire for a social and political stability without the anxiety of doubts and the necessary secrets and lies redacted in all their editions.

Outside the window of the black Audi he saw that the crowds, which had been diminishing in size in the last few days, were starting to grow again, even at one in the morning.

42.

The installation of the Goddess of Democracy statue in the middle of Tiananmen Square had the immediate effect of galvanizing the dwindling numbers of student demonstrators, and within hours of its installation they ballooned to more than three hundred thousand, including onlookers. But that number fizzled out quickly, even with the attendant stage performances and singing of revolutionary songs, followed by the ominous silence of a dwindling crowd.

By now most of the Beijing student demonstrators were exhausted and disorganized, and most of them had gone back to their campuses. Some even returned to their studies. Struggles emerged for the leading positions among the student organizations, as Wang Dan was replaced by Feng Congde as the chair of the Autonomous Federation of Students, and a call for another hunger strike failed, leaving the Square occupied mostly by the out-of-town students who were also beginning to leave Beijing.

Ge first attended the Saturday morning meeting of the six Elder members and the temporarily reduced three-member Standing Committee. At the end of this short meeting Li Peng moved that "in order to put a quick end to the turmoil and restore order to the capital," the military must move in and clear Tiananmen Square.

Deng closed this meeting by ordering President Yang to pass this decision to the Central Military Commission for immediate execution.

—I really did not want to call this meeting, Yang said, as he convened a meeting the next afternoon that included the

Commander of the Beijing Military District and deputy commander of the martial-law troops. The situation has become extremely volatile. We have to settle on some resolute measures for clearing the square. Let's begin with you, Comrade Li Peng.

Li then described what Ge wrote down in his notebook as the *counterrevolutionary riot* that started at the Muxidi Bridge in western Beijing [*Editor's note: about six kilometers from the center of Tiananmen Square.*] the previous night when a CCTV film crew driving a Mitsubishi jeep borrowed from the Fifth Squad of the People's Armed Police accidentally ran onto the sidewalk and killed three workers and injured one. Li then described how the *black hands* exploited this situation and convinced the citizens to protect their neighborhoods and set up major roadblocks at all the major intersections leading into downtown Beijing, resist martial law, surround the soldiers to keep them from moving, puncture the tires on their trucks, and confiscate their munitions and provisions.

—But we have the upper hand here, Zhang interrupted. For the last week various units of the PLA have been secretly inserting their soldiers into the center of Beijing. Some arrived in unmarked trucks, with their weapons hidden. But most came in street clothes beginning in very small groups. Yesterday a large group of well-trained troops went through the underground tunnels and positioned themselves inside the Great Hall of the People. With everything in place, Deng has ordered the Square to be cleared before dawn tomorrow, and, I repeat, there must be no bloodshed inside Tiananmen Square, period.

It was already dark when Ge arrived at the main check-point to Deng's residence at Mei Langgu Street. The first security agent did not allow him through because Ge's name was not cleared to enter that evening.

—Please call Deng's personal assistant, Wang Ruilin. I have to personally deliver those notebooks tonight, Ge said, pointing, as the the agent had already removed them from the bag for his inspection.

Even at late this hour, Deng was in his study going over files and other documents. He looked up at Ge, and invited him to sit.

—But no, please, this will be short. Then, looking directly at Deng, Ge said, I have been troubled by the turmoil of the last month, and I find that I must leave this generous and challenging position of being your notetaker, and find another way to lead a life.

Deng looked at Ge, but he did not look surprised and did not light up a Lesser Panda.

—Yes, Deng said, I saw it coming. I still trust you. Go with my best regards.

At that, Ge left the last two notebooks and removed the security clearance tags hanging from his neck and placed them on the top of a stack of papers. As Ge was about to leave the study, Deng said with a smile, perhaps I'll see you at some future *qiáopái* tournament.

44.

Ge found out the next day that while he was meeting with Deng, some advance troops of the 38th Group Army had reached the major blockade at Muxidi Bridge where they were pelted with rocks, soda bottles, bricks, and curses. Without protective shields, they sustained some injuries but maintained strict discipline, which only incited the blockaders into more aggressive tactics and who then climbed over the barricades and moved with sticks, shovels and axes menacingly toward the approaching soldiers.

Soon the troops started throwing tear gas canisters, but the resisters were prepared for that. Next came the rubber bullets that didn't slow anyone down, and then they fired warning shots into the air from their Norinco Type 68 assault rifles. [*Editor's note: the Type 68 is a knock-off of the Russian AK-47, and both use the same ammunition, 7.62 x 39 mm. Norinco stands for China North Industries Group Corporation, one of the world's largest manufacturers and dealers in weapons from small arms and land mines, up to and including main battle tanks, cluster munitions, and precision strike systems.*] They were loaded with hollow-point bullets outlawed by several international agreements. Then flanked in two rows facing the resisters, the front half kneeling, they opened fire, followed by their vehicles moving at high speed.

After some border skirmishes near the entrances to Tiananmen Square the 38th got through the six kilometers in four hours and arrived at Tiananmen Square well past midnight just in time to start clearing the Square of the one hundred

thousand citizens still left. The Taiwan pop singer Hou Diji-
an negotiated safe exit routes, and by four they started leaving
from the southwest entrances just before the troops entered
the Square and completely cleared it of demonstrators, crush-
ing the Goddess of Democracy statue by five-thirty, just before Deng's dawn deadline.

Then the body count started. Ge found as much information he could get his hands on, and then assembled the following list showing the range of estimates starting with the highest.

U.S.S.R.	10,000
Amnesty International	1,000
U.S. Ambassador James Lilley	Hundreds
Nicholas Kristof for the *N.Y. Times*	50 soldiers, 400-500 civilians
Chinese government	241

45.

Ge continued sitting at the Beijing Hotel's second-floor bar listening to the American journalists talk about the numbers. He had learned at the flea market that this was the meeting place for a foreign journalist to tell the others his narrative of what had happened that day, and then to use it when it's quoted back to him almost verbatim an hour and three drinks later by another journalist as a verified story crosschecked by a second source. Someone near Ge asked if the American Ambassador James Lilley's numbers were reliable, since he'd only been in the country for about a month, and that the previous numbers game he played when he was a CIA operative working in Vietnam would disqualify his estimates, followed by how the fuck would he know? with Ge automatically reaching for a notebook as if he were still the notetaker in the room. And another one asked about the hardships created by the huge inflation in the last two years and the influx of migrant workers into the city in the last two months.

Then someone asked who is responsible for all the deaths, and the answers around the bar were numerous. Someone suggested restricting the answers to the last month for the answers to make any sense, if there's any sense at all.

—Okay then, someone answered. The first mistake the government made was not to meet with the students early in April and start a dialogue when the students were only worried about the government's control over their future careers.

—Yeah, someone interrupted, before the Party made its second mistake with the April 26 editorial that basically forced the students to switch their demands and proclaim the need for the government to end corruption and to begin the political reform that's needed to accompany the economic reform.

But who is personally responsible? The long list included just about everyone, including the platoon leaders who handed out the hollow-point ammunition, the rural privates who loaded it into their Type 68 automatic rifles and pulled the triggers, the company commander who gave the order to fire, the student leaders who kept on flip-flopping their list of demands, Wuerkaixi who wore pajama bottoms to a meeting with Premier Li Peng, yeah, and someone said the gatekeeper at Nuremberg, another the grunt at My Lai, the top politicians who had their personal careers on the line and tried to scam each other to score points with Deng Xiaoping. At the top of the list: Li Peng, and Deng Xiaoping, who made the final decision for all of them.

—Just take them all out the southern gate to the Palace and behead them, like they've been doing for a thousand years, someone yelled, plus all the relatives, friends, teachers that they've encountered in their lives.

Just at that point the American Associated Press photographer Jeff Widener came into the bar and gave the report that a man had just tried to stop a column of tanks that had entered Tiananmen Square. [*Editor's note: that was a column of tanks from the 1ˢᵗ Armored Division of the 65ᵗʰ Group Army based in Juxian south of Beijing in Hebei Province. The tanks were the main battle tank Type 59, manufactured by Norinco in its Factory 617 in Mongolia. It was modeled after the Soviet T 54//55, the most produced tank in military history.*]

—I just used up my last roll of Fuji film and had to borrow some from Kirk...

The group of foreign journalists and photographers grabbed their notebooks and cameras and crowded into the lobby elevator and hurried to the sixth floor balconies facing the Square.

46

Back in his apartment that night, Ge was moved enough by the events around him in the past week to write a poem about his feelings, something he had not done since changing his name from G.

Walking in Beijing under Midnight Moon

Don't tell anyone this
But I feel as if I'm walking in circles
Grass glistening, smell of coal smoke drifting
On this clear June midnight

Concrete block buildings in all shades of grey
Dark figures leaning in hutongs
With less than a little money to spend
They have been here for generations, sweeping

Everywhere the carefully planted trees
Tendered rows of elms, willows and locusts
Above them the flitting magpies and higher
Always the crows that have witnessed all

And all have come to this, like me
Stones and people from every province
Still able to be astonished, still doing
Wrong or right for different reasons

The familiar, differing warm looks on their faces
Their all day tea jars warming in the sun
In the shadow of another Mao talisman
Or any other remediable mistake

148

I walk the night writing this poem
That has become important for me to remember
Holding back tears the entire distance
A loop I would bicycle to work every day

At every intersection thousands of other bicycles
Negotiate past truckloads of last fall's rotting cabbage
All that's left of any government surplus
Distributed free to every work unit

These signs now fill all of us with caution
Saying the exact same thing to each other
And to the working horses that have refused
To pay attention for centuries in their toil

Tomorrow morning I will watch the early dancers
Face the sun at the pavilion
As if they've just jumped out of prison
Onto the back of a dragon vexing everywhere

Later I will pick up a new gingko leaf
Wipe off the soot with my fingers
And press it deep into my burgundy passport
So dear, where it will stay, where I am not

[*Editor's note: written in unrhymed quatrains with variable
line lengths, this was the Jueju form popular during the Tang
Dynasty.*]

47.

The next day Ge started looking at his life after his resignation. In the last three months, Ge felt that he had been kid-
napped to play a role in someone else's novel. Now this someone—this unknown author, perhaps another letter-writer, or
a ghostwriter—was returning him to his own story, along with
his original name

What was the end, after all, after all the revelations of the
character flaws and institutional weaknesses that had accumu-
lated in Ge's notebooks that prompted his resignation, what
was the end? Who will the censors from the State Administration of Press, Publications, Radio, Film and Television as well
as from the Ministry of State Security go after? Ge had only
worked under strict directions as the personal notetaker for
the nation's preeminent leader Deng Xiaoping, after all. Will
he be placed in a cangue and trotted out the south entrance of
the Palace as a political dissident and then beheaded publicly? Or shot at a football stadium? Or disappear into Beijing's
Qincheng Prison?

And what about his notebooks? Will they be considered
a collection of false words and disappear into Zhongnanhai's
vaults? Will they be published by Beijing's Commercial Press
under the title of *The Man Who Copied Words*? Will they be
edited and then selected sections displayed in a wing of the
National Museum in Tiananmen Square so severely redacted that the readable text has no meaning, and to later travel
around the world displaying China's portable history that has
no past, present, or future, like the Xi'an terracotta exhibition?

As it was when Ge turned in a full notebook, he suspected that the verbatim transcriptions did not capture the real intent behind the speeches he recorded at these high-level meetings, even with the marginal notations. Many of them were too long, with too many lies, too many secrets, with too many irrelevant linguistic distractions, a garland of false words, deliberate leaks of coded and confusing reports, and most often, meaningless political chitchat filled with aphorisms and limpid quotations from Mao Zedong Thought.

In this end, then, Ge found there was not a single item in the stack of notebooks that he could remember at all, who said what, when, why, and especially what was really true. He was not even sure that he could do better if the notebooks were right before him. In this way, he trusted fiction more.

48.

When he was growing up, Ge's home was always filled with books. There he picked up the habit of reading, which continued when he was studying number theory at Beida years later where he took a literature course every term even as the students were decreasing from one to the next, along with their interest.

He looked at the stacks of books around his apartment and checked out his options. Given his experience as Deng's personal notetaker, he could leave China and work for the British Broadcasting Company as a correspondent, become a staff writer for the American Contract Bridge League's *Bulletin*, apply for a Nieman Scholarship and enroll in Brandeis University's investigative reporting program, apply for a residency at Stanford University's Hoover Institute, join Hong Kong's developing Umbrella Revolution, apply for a work permit to teach conversational Pǔtonghuà at an American community college, work with the Chinese evangelical Bob Fu in Midland, Texas.

Ge didn't find any interest in any of them. He wanted to remain in China, and admitted for the first time what he thought was Mao's gift to the nation, perpetual revolution. So then he decided he might quit playing *qiáopái* altogether, as he had never liked most of the players he had encountered in the game, people who didn't read and avoided talking about ideas or politics, the men obsessed with football, and their social glue of stultifying chitchat.

He decided that he would continue to learn the strategic game of Go, and move to Shanghai where he was sure he could make some kind of living that would use his probability tables, probably designing actuarial formulas for insurance companies, playing card games for money, and that he would continue to be a letter-writer for those in need.

But first he had to do two things. He removed the obsequious radical that had been added to his name, that silent vowel, and reclaimed his birth name of G, the initial of Kafka's Gregor Samsa which his parents had given him. Next he was going to take the morning G653 train to spend some time with his parents who had retired and were living at his paternal grandparents' home in Shiyan.

On the way to the rail station the next morning, G took one last look at Tiananmen Square, a goodbye kiss to Beijing.

CHAI Ling

A Peking University student and the commander-in-chief of the Hunger Strike Committee, she announced the end of the hunger strike on May 19, opposed by Wang Dan [see below]. She escaped from Beijing after June 4, took a degree in international relations at Princeton in 1993, then a M.B.A. from Harvard in 1998. She became an evangelical Christian in 2009. Her 2011 memoir *A Heart for Freedom* was published by Tyndale Momentum, a Christian publishing house.

She has been called to testify before the U.S. Congress on human rights issues in China more than ten times.

DENG Xioping

After June 4, he retired from all government positions, and died in 1997 at the age of ninety-two from Parkinson's disease.

JIANG Zemin

On June 24 he replaced Zhao Ziyang as General Secretary before becoming the Fifth President of the People's Republic of China in 1993. He retired from all government positions in 2004.

LI Peng

He retired as Premier in 1998, and monitored the construction of the Three Gorges Dam as well as the Shenzhou Manned Space Program.

KRISTOF, Nicholas

A progressive American journalist, he was stationed in Beijing in 1989 as the *New York Times* correspondent. With his wife Sheryl WuDunn, their reporting of that political spring received a Pulitzer. He won a second Pulitzer in 2006.

TANK MAN [aka Wang Wellin]

The young man who tried to stop a column of 1st Armored Division of the 65th Group Army Type 59 main battle tanks in Tiananmen Square on June 5. Photographs were taken of him by Arthur Wah of Reuters, Charlie Cole of *Newsweek,* Stuart Franklin of Magnum Photos, among others. Nine years later *Time* magazine ran Associated Press photographer Jeff Widener's shot in its article honoring the most important people of the 20th century.

An unsubstantiated rumor described the man as a nineteen-year old student by the name of Wang Wellin, who had either disappeared or had been charged with political hooliganism before disappearing from Beijing and later working as an archaeologist in the National Palace Museum in Taiwan.

In 1999, the newsmagazine *Time* honored him as one of the 100 most influential persons of the 20th century.

WANG Dan

Another freshman leader of the Autonomous Federation of Students, he was charged with counterrevolutionary propaganda and incitement and sentenced to four years of imprisonment, two of them in a cell by himself in Beijing's Qincheng Prison. He went to the United States after his release in 1993 and earned a Ph.D. in East Asian History from Harvard in 2008. Currently he teaches history of the People's Republic of China at Taiwan's National Tsing Hua University.

WIDENER, Jeff

For his shot of the Tank Man this Associated Press photographer used a Nikon FE2 camera with a 400 mm lens and Fuji 100 color negative film.

WUERKAIXI

The Uyghur freshman at Beijing Normal University and one of the Autonomous Federation of Students' leaders, he was smuggled out after June 4 to Hong Kong before being awarded a Neiman Fellowship at Harvard where he stayed for a year before moving to Taiwan. Like Chai Ling, he also became an evangelical Christian in 2002.

ZHAO Ziyang

After being removed as the General Secretary and all other appointments in June, he was placed under house arrest for fifteen years without charges in a hutong formerly owned by one of Empress Cixi's hairdressers. He died in 2005 from pneumonic complications.

158

Other June 4 Fictions

160

Cadenzas

I take the melodic line and push it past history and imagination—then I pelt it with eggs until it comes back, quick and unrelenting.

—BEETHOVEN, on the 18 cadenzas he wrote
for Mozart's piano concertos

When there was enough to fill up all the ballots in the room, Arias embraced the particulars and stood up. Believe me, it all happened so very fast no one knew for sure it wasn't an act of the imagination. *Count them,* he said, *count them to be sure this isn't something we'd find in tomorrow morning's papers.* It was just as he said, each piece of paper unfolding all our signed promises of secrecy. There was no dissension.

In a special edition the next morning, the opposition printed the story anyway, and it included specific names, dates and places for the most part as accurately as we had gathered. Arias called just before the story came on the radio and television. *We have been betrayed; we all promised to be silent, but someone has betrayed us,* he said.

I tried to tell him it'll be all right, there was no proof, no corroborating pictures to make the story credible, the republic will not panic and forget.

But Arias reminded me we didn't have any either—yet we believed these disappearances had occurred like before, much as we often place our trust in random coincidences and wild repetitions and in fact have come to expect them like children—and then he disappeared entirely, his voice trailing into thin air.

By the time of the emergency council meeting that afternoon, only four of us showed up. We sat at one end of the long conference table trying to reconstruct the details one by one, repeating them again and again, trying to be sure we had not left out anything, anything at all.

Counting

On October 1, 1949, when photographers were busily taking historical pictures of Mao Zedong proclaiming the creation of the People's Republic of China atop the reviewing stands in Beijing's Tiananmen Square, Professor Li Weibin, Mao's confidant and trusted advisor, was standing by his side. You can see him in his long coat and glasses in the photographs that were shot from the west.

Last month I interviewed him in his home in the Fragrant Hills west of Beijing, at the same location that prompted much of Cao Xuegin's Dream of the Red Chamber. More than ninety years old by most accounts, Professor Li was collected, lucid and did not make a single error of time, place or identity.

The visit extended over the entire weekend,, and as he and his granddaughter bade their farewells at the gates on Sunday evening, he confided in me his wish to see his story published as soon as possible.

—AUTHOR'S NOTE

As often as Li told Mao to be careful, the head librarian would always find out, if not today, then tomorrow, or the day after, and without warning, she would emerge from behind a stack or cart and the two of them would have to answer her same question repeated again and again: Why are you here, to work or read? If you just want to read, go home and read.

Think, think, why are you here? No answer was acceptable, she was the librarian.

After the two of them were caught in the modern history section for the third time in as many days, both Mao and Li were sacked from their library jobs, thus ending their formal education at Beida.

—You must remember we were very young then, Professor Li reminded me almost exactly seventy years later, over there, there, pointing his carved walking cane towards the city without looking.

So out of the students' dormitory the two of them carried all their belongings, bedrolls on their backs, some clothes, their *fanhes*, but mostly books secreted out of the library in their imaginations, and went into the streets that early May, 1919, looking for a place to stay. Some friends took them in, after they promised not to hold any secret meetings, a rigidly enforced covenant that was beginning to see some arrests and then disappearances.

Li knew it was doubtful the two of them would stay there long, but they were determined, not wanting to involve their friends in something irreversible. In fact, after the first two days, Li and Mao never returned, leaving everything, everything except their chance.

—Tremors, just tremors, he said. It happens here a lot.

But in 1900 there was more, but more was not enough, so that it shook again in 1911, 1918, 1928, 1935 and again in 1966. Now his granddaughter counted by his side, though he could well do it himself, his count still reliable. A doctor of the heart, she had requested a work unit transfer here to be close to her grandfather. What she counted was entirely different, if she counted at all, that she allowed me to see in her eyes just once on the second day of the interview.

After 1919, Li and Mao separated, occasionally reappearing together in the most unusual places. When Mao took his arduous hike to Shaanxi Province in the winter of 1935, Li welcomed him at Ya'an and invited him to his son's wedding. On a flight over the Hump in 1944, an American Flying Tiger mercenary pilot saw the two of them huddled in the cargo hold, planning strategy amidst the filing cabinets and Steinway CD he was hauling around China for Madame Chiang Kai-shek just on gas tank ahead of her imminent defection.

—What was he like? What was old *huxi dai you suan wei* like, standing there on that autumn afternoon at the Gate of Heavenly Peace?

—His close friends and trusted theoreticians called him Old *Garlic Breath,* Professor Li answered. His doctors advised him to quit smoking, and one warm night that summer he personally rode around the capital putting his initials on every one of the seventy-six buses still left at the depot. But on October 1, nothing else seemed to matter. He was a monument there, facing south in the tumultuous afternoon sunlight, the city thronging with a million red-and-yellow chrysanthemums. Li and his son were with him, standing to his right, basking in his limelight, but they all knew the work had just begun.

—I was born next year, Professor Li's granddaughter interrupted, her only words within my hearing that weekend.

Yes, and she would have been baptized by the bishop at Nantang had the Vatican not ordered the Chinese Catholics to stop reading Chinese newspapers and wearing red scarves, red scarves, 1966, under red banners, there suddenly appeared at Beida's south gate, teenagers all, storming the gatekeepers, chanting, grabbing the head librarian by her hair and beating her to death, along with Professor Li's only son.

Yes, his granddaughter was in middle school that year, and some of her classmates were responsible. Nevertheless she blamed Mao for doing nothing, and in two years went away to medical school to study what there was left of any healing.

—There were no benches, count them, he said, there were no benches, not one, not a single one.

We sat there counting, one empty space after another in the photograph.

Baby, come hug, come hug and say goodbye.

It reminded her of the night her father died. As she bent down to touch him that last time, there was no smell of tobacco on his breath, on the night he died.

Come baby, come hug.

Sometimes our nerves are like that, brought about by our own carelessness, ignoring storm warnings, plain forgetting, or just looking the other way for no reason at all.

—What did you think, what did you think though as you stood there next to him with your son who would soon father a daughter and then be beaten to death by her classmates before she finished middle school?

There were no benches in sight, that is to say, there were no benches. Everyone was standing up, shouting, waving tiny red flags. It's true, Pathé News was there, recording it all and then broadcasting it all over the world. Edward Murrow too, but he didn't see any benches either. Even if he had seen any he would not have mentioned it in his broadcast, since nobody in the United States would have cared.

—So why were you counting benches when you knew there weren't any on the review stands or in the Square that you couldn't see anyway?

In the past perfect tense of Chinese grammar, he suggested that while he stood there between *Old Garlic Breath* and his own son, he had anticipated this inevitable calamity. There is no other way to translate this.

What brought us back could have been anything, the granddaughter getting up to replenish our tea, a tree in the courtyard shimmering in the light, anything at all. Who was to say why the breathing stopped, if it had stopped at all? Why were our voices filled with double meanings?

—You know, he was always afraid of the cold, Professor added.

Yes, we know, though sometimes not by name, yes.

Baby, come, come say hug, come say goodbye.

The heart is such an extravagant organ.

Definitions

Shun Min was assigned the news anchoring position right after graduation from the national broadcasting institute. At three hours a day, ten days a month, no writing or editing or reporting stories, just show up in time for makeup before noon and before six to read the news, it was easy enough, the envy of his classmates who were given jobs as video librarian, station timekeeper and boom operator. For the first two years he put all of himself into his work, each story he read, however long or short and sometimes ambiguous, carried his most sincere and believable expressions, his voice pulsing with heart-felt humanity, assuring his viewers of the safe passage of another day. *Trust me, trust me,* he had said at least five hundred times a year in the privacy of four million homes, *I will not lie to you,* and the people in the capital believed him, even when the lights sometimes reflected off his glasses. On the streets he was easy to recognize, and citizens would stop him and express their trust, sometimes touching a hand or a sleeve, and once, in this country where things numinous have been banned since its liberation in 1949, an elderly woman limping on her left side lightly tugged one of his ears just to make sure he was not divinity itself.

This April when he was reading a brief story on the evening news about the student gathering at Tiananmen Square, a wisp of anxiety appeared in his eyes, and for the remaining minutes before the camera focused on the international weather map, his voice sounded distracted, then stumbled once on the temperatures between Karachi and Cairo. After the broadcast, the news producer approached him, concerned about his health and diet. The station manager offered a car to take him home. Slightly cautious from all this attention, he said *I'm all right* carefully three times before they believed him, then rode his bicycle home after wiping off his makeup going down in the elevator.

In the approaching twilight of another promising spring sunset, Shun wondered about riding downtown to see the students but, not being a reporter, he went home instead, mentally counting the number of times these students had gathered here before: 1900, 1911, 1927, 1935, 1949, 1966, 1976, and now in 1989, at least eight times this century, although he was not certain 1966 should be included.

That evening as he continued reading another novelist preoccupied with the scar on the national memory left there by the decade of political aberration between 1966 and 1976—a wound so deep that even now a generation later people still refuse to talk about it, as if it had completely vanished, or had not happened at all, which Shun knew was not true—he heard a soft knocking on his apartment door. All evening he had heard the repeating sirens of police and emergency vehicles passing in the streets and the excited voices of his neighbors who had gone to investigate the rumors but, as a news professional, he knew that such compulsive curiosity could wait until the stories came into the studio in the morning, after they had been gathered, sorted and checked by knowledgeable persons trained and experienced in interpreting the raw narratives from these dramatic events. All he would have to do was sit back and read them, all there in the past perfect tense.

A tall man in a long coat introduced himself politely, though he did not need to do this since Shun recognized him as the key member of the central secretariat's policy-making bureau. Over his shoulder, Shun could see the shapes of two other men standing in the background, away from the light in the hallway.

—I can stay only a minute, the bureau member said, let's not waste it standing on ceremony. From your broadcast to- night, we were worried about you. He paused, letting his message enough time to sink in. Then he asked, have you been wondering what's happened to the students?

—No, I don't think so, Shun answered.

—Do you think like your neighbors that some students have disappeared? That the PLA is responsible?

—No, I didn't know my neighbors thought that. I didn't even know there were any soldiers.

—Those are only irresponsible rumors uttered by peasants. You have done a famous job on television, and we want to encourage and help you, and then with both hands he flashed open the flaps of his long coat.

Its folds were lined with sheets and sheets of stamped official papers.

—Here, he said, this will help you understand our deliberated position. This is your new definite dogma on disappearance. But there's no need to read it, it's official, he added, handing Shun a sheaf of papers. It says that information transmitters such as radio, film, books and newspapers, and television, they are forbidden to convey stories about disappearances, ever. They are demoralizing: they can create turmoil and panic the people and destabilize the government and society.

—And besides, he added with some emphasis, it's not true, it's not scientific, people don't just disappear.

They both stood there a moment thinking about what had just been said. Shun could hear one of the men in the shadow thumbing a butane cigarette lighter, *click, click, click,* before it was lost in the sound of another passing siren. Before that too was replaced by the other man knocking soft but distinct on his door.

—I must go now, the bureau member said and shook Shun's hand.

After he left, Shun continued standing in the middle of his apartment until the official papers dropped forgetfully from his hand. He then spent the rest of the night in a living room chair thinking about what the bureau member had said. Was his visit a warning? It definitely was not a routine visit announcing a policy change—that would surely have gone to the station manager first, or the news director. And why me, he thought, I just read the news that's handed to me ten minutes before I go on the air. Did I betray something when I read the student story tonight? And soldiers? And disappearances? How does one read a story about disappearances, after all? Who can authenticate it, he asked himself, until he remembered some stories he had read in a grey-market American newsmagazine one day when he was waiting for someone in a downtown joint venture hotel lobby, some stories about people disappearing in green Ford Falcons in Argentina and others losing themselves in Los Alamos just before Japan surrendered in 1945. But maybe these were not the same things. Maybe, maybe, he repeated to himself until it was beginning to get light outside.

The news director wasn't in his office when Shun went to see him the next morning. All of the drawers of the news archivist's filing cases and desks were opened, however, overflowing with papers, more as if someone had stopped in the middle of trying to file them away. Shun picked up a sheet from those scattered on the floor. *Dateline Buenos Aires, August 7, 1977. Disappeared today, Pepe, Marianna and Angela Mendoza, father, wife and daughter, 27, 24, and infant, witnesses said, whisked away in a green Ford Falcon station wagon while they were walking along Avenida Florida in broad daylight. No known political activism or membership.* Shun picked up another one, a similar disappearance, Shanghai 1937, then

Selma 1977, Warsaw 1945, and on and on, the room full of it, until he got to Hiroshima and Nagasaki 1945.

Dazed, he walked into the lobby and did not see anyone there at all, only gaps where they should have been. As he started out the sliding glass doors of the station building, he noticed too that everything on the outside had entirely disappeared, all of Beijing had absolutely vanished, everything except for his exact double, another Shun Min, walking up the sidewalk to the building as if it too had disappeared. He knew this to be true, he said to himself, because he could tell this story now in the first person, a choice he did not have yesterday.

Lipstick

This man is serious. He has put a map of the Mall in my hands and is now insisting that after meeting with the media at the Washington Monument the parade/demonstration must be routed to the White House for a final statement.

—You're crazy, I shout above the other voices, a strategy I learned at Columbia's democracy salon. We'll need two permits. One from the Park Service for the Mall maybe, but the city will never give us one for Pennsylvania Avenue on the same day. Impossible.

Wang shakes his sheen of shoulder-length hair from side to side, practicing for the TV cameras. It glistens in the subdued light of the living room. It's gorgeous and its image has already been beamed via 20th Century Fox to every TV set on both sides of the Pacific. Then abruptly he looks straight at me, his seriousness and sincerity focused for the photojournalist's close up.

—Look, we're all here, Wang sweeps his arm around the crowded apartment. Even double-exiled Black Cat from San Diego.

—We know, we know, yells someone from the kitchen. Where he's been selling Yamaha guitars after his expulsion from Berkeley for lying about his Green Card. YA-MA-HA. Ha, ha, good thing he lives in California. For penance he must offer his Nanjing grandmother oranges every week.

—We must be serious here, Wang continues, Wang the career organizer, who has put this curious coalition together, COC, Committee of Overseas Chinese, ever watchful of human rights violations in China and always promoting the struggle for democracy in the motherland.

But what he says is true, we're all here, half of Beijing's leaders' children all gathered in one room in America, the third brain drain this century—Qing from Brandeis who still sleeps with the light on, Gao holding down a Nieman at Harvard, Liu from CUNY, and even Crazy Li from Michigan State. A casually tossed grenade here could seriously alter China's future, or at least China expats' future.

—We must also select someone to make the speech, that same voice yells from the kitchen.

—What about the physicist Fang Lizhi? Xiao Liu raises her hand. She is rumored to be dating an American, but she has not changed her Beijing-style bobbed hair.

—No, that won't work, Wang answers. Nobody trusts a physicist, not since Galileo.

—He isn't a physicist, you idiot, Black Cat shudders. Astrophysicist, not the same thing. But I agree with you, Fang's not very good in front of a camera, in either language, Chinese or English, astrophysics or politics.

Here comes the silence of agreement, the vast stillness of conspiracy hatched some ten years ago in Beijing, before the first gathering in front of the Gate of Heavenly Peace in April.

—We need someone younger, someone with good teeth, someone who'll make those mothers in Peoria cry over their TV dinners and send us their money before their husbands come home, Xiao Lin volunteers. Ever the consensus builder, she has not yet abandoned her role of saying what everyone else in the room is already thinking.

—All right then. What about Wang Dan?

Someone had to say it, and it is Black Cat.

—He's recognizable, even for America's short attention span. Good in front of cameras, and he sounds convincing with his new dentures. He even mentions those prisoners that have been left behind, by name. Surely that will wring some hearts for our cause.

—Yeah, but there's always that rogue reporter out there who's going to make him slip, even with an interpreter. It happened twice last year, in Milwaukee and in Denver. Wang sounds very sure of himself—he has stopped shaking his hair for this announcement.

—He's going to be our next president; we can't expose him to any negative publicity.

—What about the student who stopped the tanks during the demonstration at Tiananmen Square, asks Simon Fraser's Chen, a wannabe from the south who speaks a passable Mandarin but has been accepted because of his success at raising funds from Hong Kong's motherland candle burners.

—You mean Charlie Cole's *Newsweek* photo that's reprinted all over the world a hundred times every June 4? Black Cat asks between sucks on his funky cigarettes. I thought everyone knew he didn't stop those tanks of the 38th Army in T-Square—those four tanks were unarmed, their barrels plugged, and they stopped for him. It isn't just a squabble between interpretations. I thought everyone knew that. Strange that we've never been able to identify him. Perhaps he was a MSS agent.

—Or he was a student swiftly arrested and imprisoned, Chen argues.

—All right you two, all right, Wang intercedes, shaking his hair. Let's not fight among ourselves. We still have a lot to decide before meeting with the Park Service tomorrow.

—Hey, let's order out some Chinese, that same person yells from the kitchen. That'll get some work done.

*

Date: October 10
Time: 8:00 A.M. for staging

10:00 A.M. to 12:00 for parade, up Independence Avenue to Washington Monument

Wang, Black Cat, Xiao Liu and I are at the Park Service office filling out a form for a parade/demonstration permit. We have been here for more than an hour and are having some problems with these questions.

Organization: COC

Address:

Officers:

—Looks like you could do with some friendly assistance with that form, a woman's voice drifts to us from the blind side. A ranger with shorter hair than Xiao Liu's has come to help.

—Yes. Thanks, ma'am, Wang turns around, shaking his hair.

—Please don't ma'am me. The ranger says. I'm here to help, and my name is Dorene Okamura, she smiles, patting her burnished name plate over her starched and ironed left pocket.

Wang looks at me, but I pretend not to know what his look means. Instead I hand Dorene Okamura the form and the Park Service pen.

—This is as far as we've come, I add.

—The Washington Monument, that's okay, Fifteenth and Constitution, still within the Mall, Dorene Okamura reads the form. Let's see here. Okay so far. Hmmm.

Xiao Liu is beaming with admiration.

—October 10. Hmmm. That might be a problem, Dorene Okamura looks at me. Another group has also applied for a permit for the same time that day. Perhaps you know? Human Rights Watch, Human rights in China. AI?

—We didn't know. It is Wang who answers.

Ranger Okamura continues to talk to me, as if my running shoes, baseball hat and no cloud of tobacco stink encircling me make me less likely to misunderstand her words.

—But we can work it out, she says. They'll be going up Constitution Avenue. Would you have any problems if the two groups saw each other four blocks apart?

She is directing the question to me again, but it is Wang who answers, again.

—No problem, he says, in the same tone of voice as if the ranger had just changed her order for a Big Mac to a Double Cheeseburger. Who's their speaker, he asks.

—I think Were Kaiser, but I'm not sure.

—Yes, you mean Wuerkaixi, that Uyghur minority hooligan from Beijing Normal, that exploiter of human tragedy? I thought he was in Australia or Japan, last I heard.

—Wherever, Dorene Okamura says. But they said he'll be here October 10. 10:45 A.M. The media's been notified. My job is to see to three things: first that there'll be no conflict between the two parades; then ensure the media will have appropriate access to both groups in an orderly manner; and make sure there will be enough port-0-potties for everyone. We also provide the necessary deputized security to make sure these things will happen, and in the right order.

I can tell that Xiao Liu wants to know what a *port-o-pottie* is, but she looks down at the floor tiling instead, suppressing the question for later.

—These demonstration plans look pretty controlled and rehearsed to me, Black Cat speaks for the first time. Whatever happened to good ol' spontaneous demonstration?

—We don't believe there's ever been a spontaneous demonstration in human history. Ranger Okamura looks ready for the cameras. Not even in front of the Hilton in 1968 Chicago. In Indonesia last year, first a truck shows up with the demonstrators, then a minute later another truck loaded with rocks. They are all planned, some more successfully than others.

—If any of your people plan on being at high places, she adds, such as roof tops, monuments or trees, we must know where, when, and their names.

The four of us take turns looking at each other and say nothing.

—There'll be a staging area available to you at nine, she continues and walks to the wall map and points to a small section off the freeway at the junction of Independence and Third. Here you can organize your pro-democracy parade. Are you sure you don't know about the other group? She looks straight at Wang who is busily shaking his hair, which has become his answer to everything he wants to avoid.

Black Cat and I exchange looks to say nothing, and it is Xiao Liu who answers the ranger.

—Yes, at the staging area we can put on makeup for the cameras. Some powder so our faces won't shine under the bright lights. Some lipstick too. We must look young, energetic and dedicated to democracy.

The rest of the details are worked out quickly with the efficient ranger. Just as quickly, I lose interest in this meeting, so Dorene Okamura is talking directly to Wang instead.

*

My mind wanders back to the Beijing of ten years ago. We did it wrong back then, and we're doing it wrong again on this side of the Pacific. It's now beginning to be doubtful that we're ever going to survive the messiness of this part of our history.

But when the meeting is over, I will drive to the Georgetown Mall to look for just the right shade of Revlon. I will find the exact lipstick that will let everyone in the world know just enough, not too much, and not too little. Maybe a *Cappuccino or Natural Nude* that won't kiss off. So they will have no doubts. So they will continue to believe.

Enemy agents are found under gooseberry bushes,
and intelligence is brought by the storks.
                              —CHRISTOPHER ANDREW,
                                          Defend the Realm

I have ordered the 7th Fleet to prevent any attack on
Formosa [Taiwan].
                              —PRESIDENT HARRY S TRUMAN,
                                                June, 1950

Ever since Generalissimo Chiang Kai-shek expatriated himself to Taiwan in 1949 after a protracted civil war, his entourage and the victorious Chairman Mao Zedong had been tormenting each other over China's identity and all its Ponzi derivatives such as revenge and justice, with the U.S. 7th Fleet wearing a referee's black-and-white and patrolling South China Sea's Taiwan Strait between them to promote world peace. Occasionally they would take pot shots at each other over the hundred-and-forty miles of water separating them, an Extravagant Burst here, a Vibrant Crackle there, Sparklers and Snakes everywhere, until the aircraft carrier *USS Hornet* slipped in between them with its Rockets' Red Glare. That is, until the two coots General Cash My-check and Old Garlic Breath died within a year of each other shortly after the *Hornet* was decommissioned, and that was more than forty years ago.

Nice. Thanks for the history lesson. But that was then, this is now. What is now, and where's the story? Even a parable has a story line.

1950s. Patience. If the truth be told, the story cannot be rushed. Our engineer was the Canadian Jerry Bullock. One might say he is arguably the main player in this story, but then again such conventional interpretation is always ambiguous and misleading. In a parallel narrative, he had dreamed of designing cannons that would launch satellites into space, a huge savings over the conventional rocket propulsion. But in the 50s no one in the space industry, government, military or scientific community anywhere took his experiments seriously. Without funding then, he went into applied science's dark side and started designing and making long range artillery pieces as his day job, beginning with building a cannon for the Canadian Defence Board to fire a bullet at a speed of 4,500 miles-per-hour. In the next thirty years he did essentially the same work for about a dozen nations. Then he completely disappeared in 1990, but law officials kept it a secret for several months.

Slowly word after word the secret leaked out: because he had built the largest cannon in the world for Sadam Hussein, the HARP gun, he had been assassinated. But who did it, who gave the order and who bought the contract? Since his mercenary munitions-and-armament mortgage had been bought out by so many nations, who did it became a secret in the international intelligence community. It could have been the British MI-6, USA's CIA, or Iran's VEVAK, with Israel's Mossad as the primary party-of-interest; or it could have been an agency from Chile, Iraq or South Africa. Just about every country had a motive; everyone certainly denied it.

Finally, it was such a big secret no one knew for sure anymore, and even then doubt remained. Maybe they all wanted to stay in their lucrative intelligence business and had formed a cabal to draw straws to see who would place five bullets to Bullock's head at point-blank range in his Brussels apartment. He had worked for all of them. Maybe he did not die, and the assassination was staged to prevent more countries from improving their artillery gene pool. Maybe Bullock was still alive and sheltered in some remote international witness protection program. The only two countries that appeared to be innocent at the time were China and Taiwan, even though everyone knew the latter had been sucking on the American tit for more than sixty years.

That is until now, the Obama Decade. Nobody would have guessed at the time Pythagoras worked out his Triples Theorem $a^2 + b^2 = c^2$ amended two centuries later by Euclid's Infinite Series, $(3n)^2 + (4n)^2 = (5n)^2$ it would be hijacked into the mathematical centerpiece for calculating ballistic trajectories in a shooting war between China and Taiwan some two-thousand-and-five-hundred years later. At least this was what the cannon enthusiast wearing a card-dealer's green visor was explaining to China's People's Liberation Army political officers hunkered down over a ping-pong table in a mobile command center parked on Quemoy Island just a stone's throw above the rock-lined beach facing Taiwan.

Memories of the 1989 political spring and the Tiananmen[2] confrontations had been quietly shelved and dwarfed by the rapid economic growth of entrepreneurial capital showcased in the construction of the Three Gorges Dam on the Yangtze River, Beijing hosting the Olympics, and Shanghai's 2010 Expo. The 21st century was beginning to look like it belonged to China, its Dragon Century. During this period Taiwan had become more of an economic partner than a political adversary, even though it was purchasing huge quantities of armaments and munitions from everyone, including one-hundred-and-fifty Viper attack fighters from the U.S., just in case.

During this same period, Mao icons, statues, talismans, memorials and memorabilia both public and personal became anachronistic, along with his reputation, at least in the prosperous coastal free-economic zones. First, the party officially admitted he had erred in some of his political and personal decisions and writings, but he was still 90% correct, though no one knew for sure which was 10% and which 90%. A few years later his ratings dropped to 80. Then 75. Then 70. PLA uniform Mao badges converted to fashionable earrings started appearing in Shanghai nightclubs, first on women, then on men; first on both ears, then on one, both left and right. Taxi drivers in busy cities threw away their Mao talismans believed to prevent accidents. His image was deleted from sports trophies and chess and bridge championship medals. School-children started to forget his name, even when his image ran amok on every piece of paper currency in the country from one Yuan to a hundred, even with the identical 12.26 meters high public Mao statues in plaster, gypsum, stone, bronze or stainless steel everywhere, everywhere. [The statue itself is 7.1 meters, to correspond with the founding of the CCP on July 1, 1921; the base is 5.16 meters, to commemorate the publication date of "Guidelines for the Cultural Revolution" on May 16, 1966, and the sum of the base and the statue, 12.26 meters, reflecting Chairman Mao's birthday on December 26.]

Merchants started complaining. Not good for tourism. College students, newspaper editorials and intellectuals started complaining. Bad memory; this is not China today.

Some radical officers in the PLA and senior cadres in the CCP started fomenting a plan for the good of the country's public memory. Slowly one by one, week by week, these Mao statues started disappearing, especially from western Beijing's university row, even that supersized, twenty meters high and weighing forty-six tons stainless steel Mao in Chongqing

Medical College's front entrance. Through China's secret service, they found Jerry Bullock hiding out in Bobby Fischer's former apartment on Espergerdi Street in Iceland's capital Reykjavik and learning to play chess from the scribbled notes left by Bobby Fischer, and talked him into building another cannon, for old time's sake, just one last one, this one won't kill anyone, it'll just be symbolic, like most people's lives. And it will be easy.

The HARP gun he built for Sadam Hussein twenty-five years ago had a mammoth barrel of 500 feet and delivered a projectile 1,500 miles, five times more than what was necessary to reach Israel from Iraq. Here the distance between Quemoy and the beaches below Taichung across the Taiwan Strait, the distance was only 130 miles. Easy. Piece of cake. More like a catapult. And besides, no munitions would be involved, only the harmless public statues. Calibrating the trajectory (c^2) will be as easy as determining the hypotenuse of three points: measure the distance between the two points at right angle to each other and then entering it into the computer along with the data on the length (a^2) and weight (b^2) of the projectile. In fact, the link between the computer and the firing mechanism will also automatically calculate the current wind direction (a) and speed (b), and atmospheric variables such as humidity (($3n)^2$) and pressure (($4n)^2$). The only complication would be removing the Little Red Book (($5n)^2$) from Mao's hand on some of the statues, because its odd size would foul up the grooves in the barrel.

And by the time the US 7th Fleet responded by launching its Super Hornet attack fighters from the nuclear-powered super-carrier *USS George Washington* anchored in Tokyo Bay 1,500 miles away, or the Raptors from Guam 1,800 miles away, the show would be over. No one hurt—only Mao's feet sticking up in the air and his head buried in the sand of Taiwan's beaches.

Are we ready then, the senior PLA officer confirmed, looking down the long row of freight cars filled with Mao statues queued up on the same rail siding constructed to absorb the recoil of the brand new 100 foot long cannon barrel.

Unknown to him and Bullock and the rest of us, Taiwan had prepared itself for this paranoiac eventuality, and had been secretly working with Bullock on building a similar gun pointed at Quemoy's beaches. Like China, Taiwan had been experiencing identical problems with Old Peanut Head icons, and had in fact been collecting all his public statues in full military dress with drawn saber and sometimes peacock plumage and storing them in an unmarked and bulging warehouse waiting for some evacuation plan, just like 1949 in reverse. And just like China, a few Taiwanese military officers came up with the same idea, and with a less bureaucratic intelligence agency had in fact located Bullock in Reykjavik a few months before the mainland spooks.

So, when the shooting started, the return fire was almost immediate, and the sustained exchange devastating. Statue after statue flew across the Taiwan Strait and landed as illegal aliens. Some collided in mid-air and exploded into dust. The noise disturbed residents as far away as Fuzhou and Taipei. Some counted the number of explosions, but stopped when they reached one hundred. Like fireworks displays, the shelling ended exactly thirty minutes from the start with a 72-shot Armageddon Brocade Finale. For more than sixty years both China and Taiwan had wanted more, they wanted revenge and justice and another chance to fly its sovereign flag—the civil war was not over yet. Sometimes, just sometimes, justice is only a matter of distance; revenge, however, is only a hypotenuse to nowhere, squared or not.

In the 70s, *armies on* both *sides* of the Taiwan Strait *floated bundles of* consumer *goods* to the other's shores in order to *showcase* its *prosperity. Taiwan sent underwear, tape recorders, and biscuits* embossed *with Chiang Kai-shek's* image; and *Mainland* reciprocated with *beef jerky, tea, and Maotai liquor.*

—Evan Enos in *The New Yorker,* Oct. 11, 2010, p. 46

Acknowledgments

Besides drawing on his teaching residency in Beijing in 1989, including extended conversations with dozens of university students and professors about their experiences in their political spring, for this novel—a work of fiction—the author cross-tabulated their personal narratives against the published and often competing claims of fact in newspapers, magazines and books. Some of the references listed below contain credible factual material, including redacted material gleaned from the heavily guarded archives in Zhongnanhai, the seat of the Chinese Communist Party.

The editorial board, Beijing Publishing House; the British Broadcasting Corporation; Timothy Brook; Ian Buruma; Nien Cheng; Foreign Broadcast Information Service (FBIS), an intelligence component of CIA's Directorate of Science and Technology; *Global Times*, Xinhua News Agency; Nicholas Kristof; Marc Lambert; Li Qiao; James Lilley; Perry Link; A.R.Miles; Andrew J. Nathan; Michael Oksenberg; *Renmin Ribao*, Xinhua News Agency; Harrison S. Salisbury; the *South China Morning Post*; the (*Tiger*) *Standard;* Lawrence R. Sullivan; Mark V. Thompson; Ezra Vogel; Sheryl WuDunn; Yi Mu; Zhang Liang.

About the Author

Born in Boston and educated in the United States, Alex Kuo lived his early childhood in the French Concession of occupied Shanghai for most of World War II.

Since 1963, he has taught and directed programs and departments at several American universities, including Roger Williams, University of Colorado and Washington State, and has been appointed writer-in-residence at Knox College, Washington State and Mercy Corps.

He taught American literature in Beijing in its political spring of 1989, and has returned to it almost every year since, lecturing at Peking, Tsinghua, Beijing Foreign Studies, Beijing Forestry, Beiihang, Fudan, Jilin and Hong Kong Baptist Universities.

He has received a Rockefeller Bellagio residency, three National Endowment for the Arts fellowships, a Fulbright Scholar appointment, a Lingnan Professorship, Knox College Distinguished Alumni Award, and the American Book Award for his short fiction collection, *Lipstick and Other Stories*.

from **Reviews of Other Books by Alex Kuo**

This fast paced political thriller offers a much needed fresh and multidimensional examination of student unrest on both sides of the Pacific. By switching points-of-view Kuo shows a literary craftsman at work and proves once again that fiction counts.
—Writer, publisher, and editor ISHMAEL REED,
Conjugating Hindi

Alex Kuo is a mainstay of Chinese American and Asian American writing. He has helped to create this field by producing some of its most important work and by defining the field. His concerns are large and universal—the ecological landscape of the American West, politics, history, and, of course, human emotions. As a citizen of many cultures, he has taken on the responsibility of integrating his prodigious knowledge of many peoples.
—Writer MAXINE HONG KINGSTON,
Tripmaster Monkey

Alex Kuo's brilliant and original The Man Who Dammed the Yangtze *tells a parallel tale for our time. Global corporations and their politician minions have cometp rule. Two startled, compassionate mathematicians—one American, the other Chinese— foresee the disasters that compulsive dam building will trigger. But their compassion, insight, intelligence and calculus seem no match for the magnitude of arrogance, ignorance, ambition, and wrong-headed greed they confront. Alex Kuo's ocean-swimming, epic poem of a novel, co-locates and pinpoints the back-story to a future crisis our planet can be spared.*
—Writer, actor and musician AL YOUNG,
The Song Turning into Itself

I happen to believe that there are a lot of good poets around at present, but a poet like Alex Kuo, who possesses a highly developed moral sense and a bitter honesty, is rare at any time, and especially in this time. We need him.

—Poet CAROLYN KIZER,
Yin

from **Reviews of** *shanghai.shanghai.shanghai*

Alex Kuo is a creative outlier whose latest novel highlights the roles that fiction, nonfiction, and language play within the context of state censorship and cultural privilege. The motivating issue is China's state censorship which freezes out fictions and nonfictions so that only one official truth remains.

—ADRIENNE IP,
International Examiner

An inimitable blend of fiction, cultural satire and political romance. Imagine taking a stroll through the streets of modern day Shanghai while wearing a monocle that transmits images from a historical Shanghai, where the international settlement held on to the last gasp of its 100-year history. Kuo's most self-assured manifesto of creative autonomy to date, this book takes you around Shanghai and the Chinese mind as no other tour guide could. It's a book that I'll turn to again.

—WEN JIN,
Pluralist Universalism

Mr. Rushdie, Mr. Murakami, let me introduce you to Alex Kuo whose novel shanghai.shanghai.shanghai *moves effortlessly between China in 1939, 1989, and now. The narrator, Ge, talks to his characters and people from the past as the author crafts a course between fiction and non-fiction to find the truth about China's (and America's) modern histories. There is Lu Xun anger here at history's follies, but also unsparing satire and outrageous humor. A dazzling read, a must for Sinophiles and anyone interested in how we get our truths about China yesterday and today. After eleven previous books, this is Kuo's masterpiece, as innovative and intelligent as any writing you can find.*
—Writer and painter ROBERT ABEL,
Riding a Tiger

Alex Kuo's shanghai.shanghai.shanghai *is a tour de force that moves seamlessly through time and space, revealing different layers of the palimpsest that is the grand metropolis of Shanghai—all told from the point of view of a journalist who lives and writes simultaneously in present day freewheeling Shanghai and in the city during its wartime occupation by Japan. Kuo's novel is a poet's fever dream and stream of consciousness rumination on the eponymous city, East and West, colonialism, Hollywood, June 4th, the corruption of the nationalist government, and the vicissitudes of life in China today—in all their multivalent complexity and absurdity.*
—Poet and translator ANDREA LINGENFELTER,
Farewell My Concubine

Alex was my first writing teacher, and 25 years later is still my teacher. His vision is sure and uncompromising. I love this book.
—Writer and basketball player SHERMAN ALEXIE

At a time when most of us are racing to reduce our world to facile, 140-character tweets, Alex Kuo has succeeded once again in doing the opposite: creating a novel that celebrates complexity and challenges our most cherished assumptions about culture, politics and even writing itself. shanghai.shanghai.shanghai *is not easy reading, but it is also difficult to put aside, a book filled with passages and personages that play over and over in the mind long after the final page.*
—Medical writer and columnist PAULINE CHEN,
Final Exam: A Surgeon's Reflections on Mortality

Bouncing between 1939, 1989 and 2010 in Shanghai, Alex Kuo wisely and mischievously weaves the crazy inconsistencies, tragedies and coincidences of globalization into a dazzling narrative that thrills, enlightens, and humanizes us. One of our most gifted and audacious storytellers, who fuses Gone with the Wind, *American missionaries in China, and the 2008 Beijing Olympics to both celebrate and expose the cultural mishaps and hypocrisies of our modern world.*
—Columnist and writer AIMEE PHAN,
The Reeducation of Cherry Truong

redbat
books

For other titles available from redbat books, please visit:
www.redbatbooks.com

Also available through Ingram, Amazon.com,
Barnesandnoble.com, Powells.com and by special order
through your local bookstore.

www.ingramcontent.com/pod-product-compliance
Lightning Source LLC
Chambersburg PA
CBHW020648260626
47157CB00008B/2952